"*You do understand, don't you?*"

Carlyle spoke quietly.

"Yes, I understand."

"Then it's easier for me to ask you something—not for me, but for Emma. She likes you. I've never seen her take to someone so quickly."

"What do you want me to do?" Briony asked, with a heart full of dread.

"Be her friend until—for as long as she needs one. Let us spend some time with you. Let her pretend that you're her mother."

Lucy Gordon cut her writing teeth on magazine journalism, interviewing many of the world's most interesting men, including Warren Beatty, Richard Chamberlain, Roger Moore, Sir Alec Guinness and Sir John Gielgud. She also camped out with lions in Africa, and has had many other unusual experiences, which have often provided the backgrounds for her books!

Lucy is married to an Italian, whom she met while on holiday in Venice. They got engaged within two days and have been married over twenty-five years. Lucy and her husband live in England, with their three dogs.

Lucy Gordon is also the author of many successful romances published by Silhouette Books.

For the Love of Emma
Lucy Gordon

Harlequin Books

TORONTO • NEW YORK • LONDON
AMSTERDAM • PARIS • SYDNEY • HAMBURG
STOCKHOLM • ATHENS • TOKYO • MILAN
MADRID • WARSAW • BUDAPEST • AUCKLAND

ISBN 0-373-03410-5

FOR THE LOVE OF EMMA

First North American Publication 1996.

CHAPTER ONE

BRIONY could hear the phone ringing before she reached the outer office. She hurried the last few steps and threw open the door. As she'd feared, the office was empty, which meant that Jenny was late again, and would be in trouble with the boss unless Briony saved her. She almost threw herself across the room to snatch up the receiver. "Brackman PLC," she intoned in her best efficient voice. "Can I help you?"

"Mr. Cosway, returning Mr. Brackman's call."

Briony swallowed. She'd only worked here for two months but she knew that Max Cosway was one of the firm's best clients. Carlyle Brackman was negotiating a vital contract with him, but today there'd been no one to pick up the phone. She flicked the switch that put her through to Mr. Brackman's office, and said, "Mr. Cosway to talk to you."

"Fine. Get those figures in here fast," came the brisk answer.

"Er—figures?"

"The figures I told you to collate so that they'd be ready when he called." Carlyle Brackman clearly thought he was addressing Jenny, and he sounded impatient.

Briony looked around wildly. Figures? What figures? Then her eyes fell on a document lying on Jenny's desk and she breathed again. "Right away, Mr. Brackman."

She darted into the office, to find her boss already on the phone. He held out his hand for the papers without looking at her, and she retreated, breathing a sigh of relief, and a prayer that Jenny would arrive soon.

As Carlyle Brackman's chief secretary Jenny was supposed to be in by eight-thirty in the morning, but two weeks earlier an emotional breakup with her fiancé had left her shattered and unreliable. Briony, whose hours started at nine, had taken to coming in earlier to cover for her, if necessary. She liked Jenny, who'd smoothed her own path with their ultra-demanding boss. Besides which, she was a good listener, and Jenny had poured out her troubles freely, winning Briony's sympathy.

She'd taken less readily to Carlyle Brackman himself. It was possible to admire a man who'd single-handedly created a dynamic firm by the age of thirty-five. But it wasn't possible to like a man who talked to his staff without looking at them, and seemed to expect an almost robotic efficiency. His dark eyes dominated a face that would have been handsome had it ever been lit up by a warm smile. His tall, lean frame was more suited to an athletics track than an office.

"He works out twice a week in the gym," Jenny had explained. "He says it keeps his mind working efficiently. Efficiency's his god."

Briony had learned the truth of this. Her powerful memory and orderly mind had enabled her to stay on top of the work, and to cover for Jenny during her collapse, but it was an effort. She looked nervously at the clock. It was almost nine. Jenny had probably cried all night and then overslept, but Carlyle Brackman would have no sympathy with that. She was looking over Jenny's desk, trying to guess where the next demand would come, when the buzzer went and a voice barked, "Come in here. I have some notes for you."

Taking a deep breath, she entered his office. His dark head was bent over papers on which he was scribbling. "I've changed the figures slightly, and I've conceded Clause Eight of the contract, so you'll have to alter that, too. Get this printed out three times and send a copy to these people that I've listed, and you can also send them—" He rattled off a list. "When you've done that, come back to me and I'll have some letters that must be urgently—who the devil are you?"

At last he'd raised his head to look at her, frowning. "I'm Briony Fielding," she said. "I've been Jenny's assistant for the last two months."

"Have I seen you before?"

"Evidently not," she couldn't resist saying. "But I've been there nonetheless."

He grunted. "Where's Jenny?"

"She's—not at her desk at the moment. I can do the tasks you've outlined."

"But you haven't taken any notes," he said, looking at her bare hands.

"I don't need notes. I have an excellent memory."

He eyed her narrowly. "I hope that's not an idle boast, Miss Fielding, because I don't like repeating myself."

"You won't have to." She took the papers from his hand and left before she lost her temper.

She switched on Jenny's computer, to make it look as if she were there, but her care was wasted. Carlyle Brackman himself came into the outer office just as Jenny burst through the door. As Briony feared, she'd been crying.

"You should have been here more than half an hour ago," Brackman told her.

"I'm sorry Mr. Brackman," she gasped. "I had some problems—"

"Leave your personal problems at home," he snapped. "That's what I do, and that's what I expect my staff to do. Let this be the last time." He returned to his office and shut the door.

Briony said a very rude word.

"Oh, hush!" Jenny begged. "He'll hear you."

"Let him," she said furiously. "He's that and worse. Of course he doesn't bring his personal problems to the office because he doesn't have any. And you know why? Because he doesn't have any personal life. Because he isn't a person. He's a machine, and nothing would give me greater pleasure than to throw a spanner in his works." Her phone rang and she grabbed it. "Yes?" she asked grimly.

"Have you finished that work yet?" Brackman demanded. "Or do you need reminding of anything?"

"I don't need reminding, thank you very much. I'll be with you in a moment."

She was in his office five minutes later, placing the new contract before him. He glanced through it, then the figures, and grunted. "Perfect. You really do have a first-rate memory." He looked up suddenly and shot her a penetrating glance that made her suddenly short of breath. "What are you doing here?"

"I told you, I'm Jenny's assistant."

"What I meant was, why are you her assistant, instead of her being yours? You're not a young girl in her first job. How old are you?"

"Twenty-six."

"Then why aren't you further up the ladder?"

"I started late. I had—family commitments."

"What kind?"

She hesitated. "I'm sorry, Mr. Brackman, but that's something I can't discuss."

"You're not married, are you?"

"No."

"Engaged?"

"No."

"Looking after elderly parents?"

"I have no living family," she said in a tight voice.

"So if I offered you Jenny's job, there are no longer any 'family commitments' to stop you taking it?"

"No, but something else would."

"What?" he asked impatiently.

"Honor. Loyalty. Jenny's been kind to me, and I'm not going to stab her in the back just because she's going through a bad time."

"Everyone goes through a bad time—"

"Will you let me finish? She was a first-rate secretary to you before this happened, and if you'll be a little patient, she'll be first rate again. It's inexcusable for you to threaten her job because she's unhappy—"

"*That will be all, Miss Fielding.* Kindly leave and get back to your job—while you still have one."

She got out of his office quickly, afraid of what she might say if she let rip. It wasn't like her to lose control, but his persistence about her family had touched a painful nerve.

It was true that she had no living relatives, but until a few months ago Briony had had a sister, a laughing, mischievous little imp called Sally. She'd been left her sole guardian when their parents died, and she'd settled for a life of temporary work so that she could be there when Sally needed her. It wasn't the brilliant career she'd once hoped for, but she did it without complaining. Sally's sunny nature had made everything worthwhile.

And then the little girl had come home saying she felt poorly. Briony had diagnosed a heavy cold and put her to bed. But the "cold" had turned out to be meningitis, and within two days Sally was dead, leaving Briony devastated and guilt-racked.

The horror of wondering what might have happened if she'd been worried sooner was something that would never leave her. The doctors had told her she was not to blame. Meningitis was hard to spot at first. But their kindly words had failed to comfort Briony, and at first the feeling of guilt had almost broken her. Gradually, however, her strong mind had fought its way back to normality, leaving only an aching misery behind. Now she walked and talked and functioned like anyone else, but the wound would never heal.

Until now she'd never noticed that her life had left her a bit of an oddity. She had a considerable gift for business, but at twenty-six was still doing temporary work. She was attractive, with a tall, slender figure, long, honey-colored hair and blue eyes that could glow with emotion, yet there was no man in her life. She'd had brief relationships that had foundered over her need to find baby-sitters before she could go out. And there'd been one man she'd almost fancied herself in love with until he informed her that there was no chance of marriage while she "had a brat in tow." He'd been out of her front door before he knew what was happening to him. Nobody and nothing was going to separate her from Sally. But in the end, something had.

She and Jenny worked steadily at their desks until lunchtime, then sent out for sandwiches and went on working. Carlyle was at his worst, piling work onto them and insisting it must be done by two o'clock, when he would be leaving.

"For this relief, much thanks," Briony muttered, clattering away at her keyboard and mentally consigning him to perdition.

At last the work was done and in his hands. Jenny slipped out for some fresh air, and Briony was free to lean back in her seat, stretching her cramped limbs. As she was enjoying a long yawn the outer door opened and a child's head appeared.

She was a little girl with fair, curly hair. Anyone else would have been charmed, but Briony had to suppress a flinch. The child was about eight, the age at which Sally had died, and her shining, mischievous smile was just like Sally's before her smile had died forever.

There was no other similarity. Sally had been a robust tomboy, and it had been reflected in her blunt, cheerful features. Although this child wore jeans, T-shirt and trainers, the outfit was topped off by a pretty, delicate face. They weren't really alike at all, but for a moment the pain was almost more than Briony could cope with.

"Hello," said the little girl.

Briony pulled herself together. "Hello."

"I'm Emma. Can I come in?"

She was in before the words were out, evidently sure of her welcome. Briony cast a nervous look at the door to her boss's office.

"I'm Briony," she said.

"I didn't see you when I was here before," Emma observed. "Are you new?"

"Yes, I've only been here a couple of months."

"Where's Jenny?"

"Oh, you know Jenny. Are you her niece or—?"

"Oh, no. She's my friend. She taught me to embroider."

"I'm afraid you've missed her. She went out for some fresh air, and to get away from—" Briony indicated the inner office door with her head and Emma giggled in perfect understanding.

"Is he very bad today?" she whispered.

"Like a fiend," Briony said in a low voice. "I'm glad I shan't be working for him long. I don't know how Jenny stands it." She supposed she shouldn't discuss her boss with outsiders, but Emma seemed to know all about him. And besides, Briony wasn't in a mood to be charitable to Carlyle Brackman.

"I didn't think little girls did embroidery now," she observed. "I thought it was all pop music and computer games. My—a girl I knew once never did anything that involved sitting down, if she could help it."

"Sometimes I haven't been very well," Emma said with a wry look that was too old for her years. "So the doctor said I had to have 'quiet pursuits.' But I'm all right now."

Briony could believe that she'd been poorly. An air of fragility still hung about her. But it was belied by the glee in her eyes as she said, "I'm going to the funfair this afternoon, and I'm going on *all* the rides."

There was plainly something significant about this. Briony caught her eye and echoed, "*All* the rides?"

"*All* of them," Emma said firmly. "Not just the easy ones that 'won't tax my strength' but the Big Dipper and the Wall of Death and the thing that goes right up into the sky and then swings you down so that your stomach gets left behind and—don't you like that kind of ride?" She was looking anxiously at Briony who'd turned pale and closed her eyes.

"I'm afraid I don't," Briony said faintly. "The Dodgem Cars are about as much as I can manage."

"Don't you like funfairs?"

"I love funfairs," Briony said. "But I never get any time to go to them. Too much work." She indicated her desk.

Emma looked anxious. "Am I being a pest?"

"Of course not."

"Are you sure? Daddy says I mustn't pester people because not everyone likes little girls."

Briony forced herself to smile. "I like them."

"Do you have one of your own?"

"Not now," Briony said after a painful silence.

She was afraid that Emma would ask more questions, but the little girl was quiet, and Briony saw that she was being regarded gravely out of a pair of dark eyes that seemed to belong to a wise little old lady. This was no ordinary child, she realized. She understood that there were things that couldn't be said.

The next moment Emma was an excited little girl again. "I wish time would move faster," she complained. "I want to go to the funfair now."

"It'll still be there," Briony promised.

Emma looked conspiratorial. "It might run away," she whispered dramatically.

"Not today," Briony whispered back, entering into the spirit. "It'll wait for you to go there this afternoon. *Then* it'll run away."

Emma laughed out loud, her little face beaming with delight.

"Shh!" Briony begged. "Don't make so much noise." Her boss was already mad enough at Jenny. If he came out and found Jenny's unruly little friend in the office it would be the last straw.

"Why not?" Emma demanded, still in a stage whisper.

"Because an ogre lives behind that door," Briony said, pointing. "And you'll wake him."

"Oo-oh! Is he a terrible ogre?"

"Terrible and wicked!"

"Is he the worst ogre that ever was in the whole world?"

"The worst that ever was in the whole universe," Briony said firmly.

It was the wrong thing to say. Emma giggled gleefully. To Briony's horror the door opened and Carlyle Brackman stood there. She groaned. Now they were all in the soup.

But before she could move to protect Emma from her boss's wrath the child let out a squeal of joy, cried "Daddy!" and rushed across the room to jump onto him. He gasped slightly as her arms tightened about his neck, and lifted her off the floor, holding her firmly.

"It's not an ogre, it's Daddy," Emma squealed.

"So I'm not an ogre today," he said, grinning. "Last night, when I wouldn't let you stay up late, I was a 'mean monster.' And that, madam, was the kindest thing you called me."

Emma chuckled and snuggled against him, a picture of happiness. Briony stared in disbelief. Was this smiling man really Carlyle Brackman? The name and general appearance were the same, but the face was transformed. This was a human being, who could look pleased when a little girl ruffled his hair and rumpled his shirtfront. This was a man who could inspire a child's adoration. Definitely it couldn't be Carlyle Brackman.

"What have you been doing out here?" he demanded. "Making a nuisance of yourself I suppose?"

"No I haven't," Emma said determinedly. "I've been talking to Briony, and she *does* like little girls, and she says you're the worst ogre that ever was in the whole universe.''

There was a short silence, during which Briony waited to be fired. But he merely frowned at her. ''You're Miss...er?''

''Fielding,'' Briony said, a slight edge on her voice.

''Yes, I remember. Your work is excellent.''

He recalled work but not names, she noted crossly. It was clear that personalities made no impact on this man: except for one personality, the eager little daughter hugging him now. Briony watched as he set her gently down, and thought she saw an odd look on his face when Emma's head was turned away. His delight in his child was real enough, but it had something uneasy about it, as though a shadow hung over them. That, Briony thought, was more like the Carlyle Brackman she knew.

''Are you ready to go?'' Emma demanded.

''No,'' he said. ''I've got a thousand things to do—''

''Daddy!''

He grinned. ''I guess they'll have to wait until tomorrow. Come on, let's have a wonderful time.''

''And Briony,'' Emma said. ''She can come with us, can't she?''

''*I* really do have a thousand things to do,'' Briony protested.

''No you don't,'' Carlyle told her unexpectedly.

''But you said—''

''Never mind what I said then. Listen to what I'm saying now. Your only job is to take my orders, and my orders for this afternoon are to come to the funfair.'' Then, as she stared in astonishment, he grinned again and said, ''No, I haven't gone mad. Emma wants you, and that settles it for me.''

"But the office—"

"Yes, it would be better if Jenny had returned. Never mind. Get one of the assistants in and tell her—" But at that moment Jenny entered. "That solves the problem," Carlyle said. He tried to address Jenny over Emma's boisterous greeting, and was obliged to order his daughter to hush, which did nothing to depress her high spirits.

"Tom will be waiting," Emma said at last.

"And we mustn't keep Tom waiting," Carlyle agreed. Taking her hand, he indicated for Briony to leave the room ahead of him. "Tom does odd jobs for me," he explained. "Today he's acting as driver. He brought this imp to the office and when we get to the funfair we'll leave him with the task of parking the car while we enjoy ourselves."

Tom turned out to be a bull of a man with a broad, good-natured face. "This is Miss Fielding," Carlyle told him. "Emma dragooned her into coming with us, but it's under protest, isn't it, Miss Fielding?"

If this hadn't been Carlyle Brackman she might have suspected he was being humorous. Then she saw him looking at her with raised eyebrows and realized that the impossible was possible. He was actually making a joke.

"Not at all," she said with dignity. "I love funfairs."

"See?" Emma nudged her father with her elbow.

"Get into the car," he ordered with mock ferocity. "Or we'll miss everything."

"Oh, no," Emma said at once. "Briony says it won't run away until after I've been."

"And, if Briony says it, it must be true," Carlyle agreed. "Now, will you please get into the car?"

Emma jumped into the front seat beside Tom, leaving Carlyle and Briony to get in the back. It was a luxurious car with a pale gray interior and plenty of leg room.

"Sorry about this," he said wryly as they began to move.

"Not at all. It's better than being cooped up in an office all day."

"With an ogre," he supplied.

Briony colored. "Look, I didn't mean—"

"Of course you did," he said affably.

"Well, I'd never have said it if I'd known she was your daughter," Briony said desperately.

"Naturally you wouldn't. Just think that I might have missed hearing the truth about myself for the first time."

"Oh, surely not for the first time," she replied with some asperity. "I imagine you must know it by now."

"Certainly I do, but I don't get it said to my face. It's an interesting experience. But you'll agree that I'm not being an ogre now?"

"You're like a totally different person now," she said in wonder.

"Human, you mean?" he challenged her wryly.

"Well—yes—since you put it that way—human."

"As opposed to an ogre in the office?"

"I think robot would be more correct," she said with a touch of demure mischief.

His grin illuminated his face again. Now that it was beamed onto her she could see how delightful it was, and she laughed out loud. He laughed with her. It was a marvelous sound, rich and bass, with a vibrancy that made her sharply aware of him as a man. His eyes were gleaming with an expression she'd never seen before, and suddenly she had difficulty in getting her breath.

Then Emma leaned over from the front seat and said, "It's going to be *fantabulous*."

Carlyle laughed and told her to sit straight, and, to Briony's relief, the dangerous moment was past.

CHAPTER TWO

THE funfair was exactly what a funfair should be, a riot of gaudy color and flashing lights, with plenty of cheerful noise. Tom dropped them at the entrance and drove off to find the car park. "Where do we start?" Carlyle demanded.

"Everywhere." Emma sighed happily. "The Big Dipper and—"

"No Big Dipper," he said at once, to Briony's relief. "The doctor said nothing too energetic."

"But going on the Big Dipper isn't energetic at all," Emma assured him, wide-eyed. "All you have to do is sit there. Just sit there. You don't actually have to do anything."

This novel view of the matter made Carlyle and Briony catch each other's eye, slightly aghast. Sensing she'd caught them off guard Emma pressed her advantage home.

"You don't have to stand up or run about, or jump up and down—" she explained.

"You are not going on the Big Dipper," Carlyle repeated gamely.

"You don't have to do handstands, or cartwheels—"

"Emma—"

"You don't have to sing or dance, or anything. You just have to *sit* there, and *sitting* there doesn't take any energy," Emma finished triumphantly, evidently having explained the matter to her own satisfaction.

19

Briony turned her head away and for a moment her eyes were blurred. Here was another likeness to Sally, who had also possessed a childlike, ruthless logic that enabled her to keep on and on until she'd driven her opponent onto the ropes. Briony had conceded many an argument through sheer weariness.

Then she pulled herself together. This was Emma's treat and she wasn't going to spoil it. She smiled at Carlyle and said, "Why don't you just give in and take her on the Big Dipper?"

"You take her," he responded so promptly that Emma giggled.

"Daddy's scared," she whispered conspiratorially to Briony, just loud enough to be overheard.

"Scared stiff," he agreed affably. "You're not going on that thing, with me or without me. So hush up, and let's have some ice cream."

Recognizing the voice of authority Emma subsided and turned her attention to the various merits of chocolate and vanilla. Having decided on chocolate, she said, "And one for Briony."

"I don't think—" Briony began, and faltered under Emma's disappointed gaze.

"Don't you *like* ice cream?"

"Yes, I do," Briony said firmly. "I like ice cream very much indeed. I'll have vanilla please."

They wandered happily among the stalls and rides, arguing the merits of each. Briony felt a small hand slip into hers, and glanced down, but Emma didn't return her look. She was gazing entranced at a fearsome machine that hurled chairs around in the sky, while all the time her hand clutched Briony's in a gesture that was clearly unconscious. Briony's heart was touched.

Suddenly Emma exclaimed, "Daddy, look!" and flung out an arm, spraying ice cream around. They all followed her indication to a shooting arcade where a sign proclaimed that three bull's-eyes would win the top prize. Hung about the stall was a plethora of fat, furry penguins. "Aren't they beautiful?" Emma breathed.

"You're a bit old for a toy like that, aren't you?" Carlyle suggested.

His daughter eyed him and for an uncanny moment Briony could see the likeness between them. It lay not so much in feature or coloring as in an expression in the eyes that spoke of a determination to get their way, directly if possible, by cunning if necessary. At last Emma sighed. "Sorry, Daddy. It wasn't really fair of me to ask you."

"Why not?" he asked unwisely.

"Well, *three* bull's-eyes," she said. "It's impossible, isn't it?"

"How much?" Carlyle demanded of the stall attendant. As he reached into his pocket for the money he became aware of Briony making choking sounds. "Miss Fielding, if you don't stop laughing right now, you're fired."

"Well, you walked right into the trap, didn't you?" she said defensively.

"I'm fully aware of that."

"But you should be pleased. Think what a tycoon Emma will make later if she can ambush you so skillfully now. In a few years you'll be able to hand over the business to her with an easy mind."

A change seemed to come over him. The summer sun was as bright as ever, but a light had gone out of his face, leaving it bleak and shadowed. He turned away and lifted the rifle to his shoulder. Briony stared, wondering what she'd said to produce that reaction.

He got the first bull's-eye, then the second, but failed on the third. "Again," he growled, handing over the money. "Everybody please be quiet."

They both fell obediently silent, but Emma and Briony caught each other's eye, exchanging silent laughter until Carlyle's glare stopped them. He raised the rifle and fired, but this time he only achieved one bull's-eye.

Emma pulled at his sleeve. "It's all right, Daddy. I knew you couldn't really do it," she said with suspicious innocence.

"You'll go too far young lady," he growled, paying for a third go.

Again he managed the first two bull's-eyes, but as he raised the rifle for the third attempt his nerve failed him.

"Couldn't I just buy the penguin for you?" he pleaded.

"That wouldn't be the same," Emma said inexorably.

"Naturally it wouldn't," he muttered. "What was I thinking of?"

It took him five attempts but he managed it at last. Emma opened her arms to receive a fat penguin, that she cuddled blissfully. "You are clever, Daddy," she rewarded him, and to Briony's delight Carlyle Brackman grinned and looked sheepish. But Emma had more terrors in store for him.

"Now Briony," she said.

Carlyle's grin faded abruptly. "Briony what?"

"You must win one for her, too."

"No thank you," Briony said hastily.

"But you must have something," Emma persisted. "It's not fair otherwise."

"I'll have a whale," Briony said, thinking fast. "They've got some lovely whales on that stall over there. A *little* whale."

As they headed for the stall, Carlyle muttered, "It's not the top prize is it?"

"No, it's the booby prize. You're quite safe."

The words were out before she could think about them, and she turned alarmed eyes toward him. But he was laughing. "Nice one," he said.

He won her a small whale on the first attempt. "Now we've both got something," Emma said happily. "What are you going to call him?"

Briony gave the matter serious consideration. "Oswald," she said at last.

"That's a lovely name."

"What are you going to call your penguin? Percy?"

"No. Oswald."

"But Briony's whale is Oswald," Carlyle said.

"I know."

"They can't both be Oswald," he objected.

"Yes, they can," Emma said in a voice that settled the matter.

"Certainly they can," Briony told Carlyle severely. "You should have known that."

"Of course I should," he said at once.

Tom appeared, having parked the car, and eating a toffee apple. Emma promptly begged for one.

"But you've only just finished the ice cream," Carlyle protested.

"But I haven't had anything else since breakfast," she said forlornly.

"It was an enormous breakfast."

She sighed and looked starving. "I've forgotten it."

"Tom." Carlyle reached for his money. "Toffee apples."

"Not for me," Briony said quickly. "It's years since my stomach could cope with toffee apples and ice cream in quick succession. I think you need to be under ten years old."

"I agree," he said with feeling.

As the afternoon progressed it became clear that Emma was a child of more than usual intrepidity. Left to herself she would have sampled all the most hair-raising rides, plus the Ghost Train. Only after determined argument did Carlyle manage to steer her toward an innocuous carousel, and then his suggestion that she ride safely on one of the inside horses was treated with the contempt it deserved. Emma installed herself firmly on the outside row, and patted the saddle behind her, with an inviting smile at Briony. The two men were left behind on the ground, holding the Oswalds.

"Next time you'll take him with you," Carlyle informed his daughter when he returned her property, adding quickly, "He prefers it that way."

Emma gave him a fond look, but it was Briony's hand she took, and Briony whom she dragged eagerly to the Hall of Mirrors. Inside the distorted mirrors threw back monstrous reflections of the four of them, making them all shout with laughter. But Briony's acute ear had detected something about Carlyle that didn't quite ring true. He joined in the laughter, but conscientiously rather than with a full heart. His love for his daughter was obvious, but Briony had a strange feeling that he was making a determined effort to be a good father, rather than enjoying her company spontaneously. It was nothing she could put her finger on, but it nagged at her.

When they emerged, blinking into the sunlight, she suggested a cup of tea.

"I thought a little later," Carlyle said.

"Yes, but there's an outdoor café over there with plenty of places free. And we're going to need lots of room."

He frowned but followed her directions, and instantly realized her wisdom. Emma insisted on treating her penguin with full honors and assigning him a chair of his own. She'd have claimed a chair for the whale, too, but for Briony, who, with admirable presence of mind, asserted that the two Oswalds would be happier together.

"You knew that was going to happen, didn't you?" Carlyle asked, looking at her with appreciation.

"I could make a good guess. She adores that penguin. I've no doubt that by now she's invested him with a full personality."

In fact Emma had gone further. In her mind both the penguin and the whale were individuals with likes and dislikes, and even a source of dispute between them. "They both like shrimps, and they keep eating each other's," she explained confidentially. "And they get *very* cross."

Luckily, since both Carlyle and Briony were rendered speechless, Tom filled the breach, asking intelligent questions about their furry companions, which Emma answered in detail. She consumed lemonade and cream buns, then turned her attention to the boating lake alongside them, filled with colorful little motorboats shaped like cartoon characters. After a while she begged for a ride.

"I'll take her," Tom offered.

Emma scrambled down, seizing the two Oswalds in her arms.

"You're not going to take them in a boat," Carlyle protested.

"They want to ride, too," Emma assured him. Carlyle regarded her helplessly.

"Don't worry," Tom said. "She'll be safe with me."

"But will he be safe with her?" Briony murmured as they watched the other two make their way to the entrance to the lake. "What would you offer against the chance of her persuading him to go on the Big Dipper?"

"She'll try," Carlyle agreed. "But she won't succeed. Tom knows it's more than his job is worth."

They watched as their companions secured a boat and began to chug around the lake, with the penguin upright between them. Emma had the little whale in her hand and was making swooping movements over the water.

"Heaven help me!" Carlyle groaned. "She'll drop that thing into the water and I'll have to win another one. Oh, what does it matter? It's been a good day."

"Yes, she's really enjoyed herself," Briony said, watching Emma tenderly.

Slightly to her surprise he seized on this. "She has, hasn't she?" he said eagerly. "She's had a wonderful time."

"It was good of you to bring her yourself," Briony said with a touch of curiosity. "Many men with your commitments would have left it to Tom."

"You mean, you're surprised that I didn't?"

"Well—yes."

"Emma is different to everything else in my life."

"More important?" she encouraged.

"Yes. More important."

"Doesn't she have a mother?"

"My wife died when Emma was a week old."

"Poor little soul. You mean, she's never had a mother?"

"Never. My female relatives have all rallied round wonderfully. She's got aunts and grandmothers who love her. But it's not the same. I've tried to be mother and father to her, but I'm not very good at either, I sometimes think."

"But she adores you, so you must be doing something right."

"I hope so. But that doesn't mean I always know what I'm doing." He regarded Briony. "I dread to think what today would have been like without you. You saw that Oswald business coming a mile off."

She smiled. "When I was Emma's age I had four dolls all called Saucepan."

"Saucepan?"

"I simply liked the name." Briony gave a reminiscent chuckle. "I drove my parents mad. I remember going out in the car with my father one day, and at the last minute insisting that Saucepan came with us. Dad said, 'Which one?' I said, 'Saucepan,' and he said, 'Yes, but *which* Saucepan?' I didn't know what he meant, because to me it was obvious that when I said Saucepan I was talking about all of them. My mother had to explain it to him. It was obvious to her, too."

"Well, I guess it's not so easy for a father to follow what's going on in a little girl's head," Carlyle observed with a sigh.

"Do you find that often?" Briony asked sympathetically.

He gave a wry smile. "It can be like talking to someone from another planet." He leaned back suddenly and regarded her with appreciation. "I guess you really do know what it's all about. I can't believe that you have no family. You act like a woman with a dozen nieces."

"I told you, I used to be a little girl myself," she said lightly. "There's no mystery about it."

"Now you're putting me off. I wonder why."

Briony stiffened. "I see no need to talk about this," she said in a tight voice. "If you think I can be helpful with Emma, I'm glad, but I won't discuss my private affairs."

For a moment a scowl darkened his face. *"Miss Fielding—"* he growled, then stopped himself impatiently. "I'm sorry. It's been so long since anyone snubbed me that I've forgotten how to cope. I had no right to pry. Please forgive me."

There was genuine warmth in his smile, which seemed to reach out across the table and touch her. Nature had given his mouth a sensual curve that she could appreciate now that he wasn't barking orders at her. She drew in her breath, alarmed at this man's impact. There was an intensity about him that left her slightly stunned. She was suddenly convinced that everything he did— whether loving, hating or suffering—would be done intensely. He had charm, too, not the emollient kind, but a rough vitality that filled the world with excitement and made her feel alive all over.

"Miss Fielding?"

"Briony," she said mechanically.

"Briony, I asked you to forgive me and you went off into a dream."

"I'm sorry." She pulled herself together. "Yes, of course, it's all right. It's fine. Honestly." With dismay she realized that she was babbling, and pulled herself together. To her relief his attention was taken with ordering them some more tea. She looked away, feeling self-conscious, hoping that her moment of awareness of him as a man hadn't shown in her face.

"Emma's adorable," she said, seeking a safe topic.

"Yes, I know," he said simply.

Briony was annoyed with him. She was doing her best to make polite conversation and he wasn't helping. Even the compliment to his child hadn't made him smile. If anything the shadowed look on his face had deepened.

"I wonder if you aren't a little too protective of her," she went on determinedly. "I understand about the Big Dipper, but some of the other rides you've vetoed would surely be all right. That Mini Dipper over there, with the dragon cars, looks safe enough." A desire to get under his skin made her add, "I'll go with her if you're scared."

That got him, she was glad to note. His eyebrows shot up. "Are you trying to annoy me Miss—Briony?"

"To tease you a little, perhaps. This is a funfair. You're supposed to look cheerful."

"I'll look cheerful when Emma returns."

"You mean, you'll switch it on for her. Actually your mind is seething with worry about how the office is managing without you. I'm surprised you didn't bring your mobile phone to keep in touch."

"That would have spoiled it for her," he said seriously.

"You're spoiling it for her by wrapping her in cotton wool."

"You don't know what you're talking about," he growled. Then he made a sound of impatience. "I'm sorry—again. I seem to do nothing but apologize to you for my bad manners. Try to ignore them, if you can. I do have a lot on my mind, but it's not what you think."

Before she could answer, Emma returned, bouncing into her chair, beaming happily. Briony noticed how

Carlyle's face immediately brightened for her, as though he were suddenly on duty again.

"Daddy, there's some Dodgem Cars over there," Emma said. "Can we go on them?"

"Darling, I don't think—"

"Oh, please, Daddy, *please*. You haven't let me go on anything really exciting."

"We've just been on the lake," Tom protested.

"Yes, but that's not *exciting*," Emma explained. "Not unless the boat has a hole, and it sinks. And it didn't," she added, sounding disappointed.

"Poor Tom." Briony laughed. "He wouldn't have gone with you if he'd known what you call fun."

"But *you'd* like to go on the Dodgems, wouldn't you?" Emma appealed to her. "You'd like it best of all."

"Yes, I think I would," Briony said with a defiant look at Carlyle.

"*Please,* Daddy." Emma supplicated her father with a look strongly suggestive of a neglected orphan.

"All right," he said reluctantly. "But look—"

The rest of his words were lost. Emma was already scampering away with the long-suffering Tom in tow. By the time Carlyle and Briony caught up, the other two had bagged a car and Emma was yelling, "Daddy, you go with Briony, and Tom and me will bash you and bash you."

"Thank you, darling," he yelled back at her. He looked at Briony. "I hope you're ready for this."

She knew Dodgem Cars were cramped, but she'd never appreciated just how cramped until she found herself sharing the tiny space with him. It was a struggle to seem indifferent as his body was pressed close to hers. She could feel the warmth of his flesh right down from her shoulder to her waist, her hips, and along the line of her leg. She wanted to pinch herself to believe that this was happening. Only this morning she'd been abusing him as a heartless monster. But that was hours ago, and in those hours the world had turned upside down, making her electrifyingly aware of his masculinity, and thrilled by the enforced contact. She tried to keep her breathing steady, and concentrate.

"Will you drive or shall I?" Carlyle demanded.

"You. I'll watch out for attack. I think it's coming now."

Sure enough, Emma, eyes wide with excitement, was bearing down on them. "That's not fair," Briony called. "Let us get started." The last word was jerked out of her as the cars collided. Their tormentor sped off, but only to turn for a renewed assault.

Carlyle managed to get their car out into the center of the rink and execute a few dodging movements, but Emma came zooming at them again.

"Got you!" she yelled.

"Look, there isn't room for two pairs of shoulders in this thing," Carlyle said breathlessly. "You drive and I'll put my arm round the back."

She found herself enclosed in the circle of his arms. For a moment she was flooded by self-consciousness, but almost immediately the moment passed as Emma came flying toward them and she had to concentrate on evasive action. She turned and began to head in Emma's direction, but Carlyle said quickly, "Don't hit Emma's car. And try not to let her hit us."

It was easier said than done. Emma had none of her father's compunction and rammed whenever she had the chance. Briony twisted and turned, but without much success, and by the time they got out she felt as if all her bones were shaking.

"I think it's about time we went home now," Carlyle said.

"Oh, no, Daddy, please let's stay a little longer," Emma begged. *"Please."* She clutched Briony's hand tighter as though relying on her for support.

Carlyle went down on one knee before her. "Look, darling, you can't—" He broke off suddenly as Emma's eyes closed. She forced herself to open them at once, but they closed again and she began to sway. "Daddy," she whispered.

"Tom, get the car," Carlyle said harshly. The next moment he'd swept his daughter up into his arms and began striding away. Briony was forced to go, too, for Emma's hold on her hand hadn't relaxed.

Tom raced ahead and brought the car down to meet them. Briony followed Carlyle and Emma into the back. On the journey home he sat with Emma on his lap, enfolding her protectively in his arms. The child's head rested on his shoulder, her eyes were closed and she looked frighteningly pale.

"What's the matter?" Briony asked in alarm. "Is she ill?"

He didn't answer in words but with a frown and a shake of the head. It wasn't a denial of her suggestion, but a command to wait until later.

"The car phone's on your side," he said. "Would you please dial a number I'll give you?"

She did so, and offered him the receiver, but he only tightened his arms about his daughter and indicated for Briony to hold it to his ear. When he answered, it became clear Carlyle was talking to a doctor's secretary. "She just keeled over," he said. "It's only tiredness—I'm quite—fairly sure of that. It's happened before—it's just tiredness. But I'd like Dr. Carson to—thank you. We'll be home in ten minutes."

He nodded for Briony to replace the receiver and leaned back, closing his eyes. His brow was damp and his face had the same dreadful look she'd seen on it earlier. She felt her heart begin to thump painfully as an appalled suspicion dawned on her. Emma had spoken of having been "not very well," as though her illness was in the past. But it wasn't. The sight of her drooping figure was enough to confirm that she was still very sick. And that terrible expression on Carlyle's face! No parent ever looked like that about a child unless...

Briony felt as though she were choking. She couldn't face this. She'd been through the valley of the shadow and seen the darkness claim one little girl. The misery and horror had almost overwhelmed her, but somehow she'd emerged. Now she was being pulled back in and it was more than she could stand. She had to get out of this car, she thought wildly. She'd make some excuse— anything—but she had to get away.

"Thank God we're here," Carlyle said as the car drew up outside a large house, set well back from the road and almost concealed by trees.

"Mr. Brackman, I—"

"Can you help me get her out?"

Briony had no choice but to do as he asked. As he lifted the child again, she tried gently to get her hand free, but Emma held on, as though even in her semi-conscious state she knew that this one contact mattered.

"Come in and help me put her to bed," he said curtly.

Silently she followed him into the house and up the wide stairs to Emma's bedroom. A middle-aged woman with a kindly face looked in. "My Tom said she'd been taken poorly," she said.

"At the fair," Carlyle told her. "The doctor should be here at any moment. Watch for him at the front door and show him straight up."

"I think I hear him," she said, and vanished.

She returned a moment later with an elderly man. Emma's grip had relaxed at last, and Briony drew away. Carlyle seemed unaware of her, but as she reached the door he said abruptly, "Wait for me downstairs."

Reluctantly she complied. Part of her still longed to escape, but a stronger part of her needed to stay and hear how Emma fared. She was followed down by Tom's wife, who introduced herself as Nora, and offered to bring some coffee.

Briony drank it alone in a large room overlooking the front garden. It was expensively furnished in a style that was up to date without being aggressively modern, but for her taste it was too neat. There was no cheerful clutter to suggest that a child lived here.

At last she heard the doctor coming downstairs, and Carlyle letting him out. When the front door had closed there was total silence for a long moment, then the sound of footsteps coming near until Carlyle burst into the room. He went straight to the drinks cabinet, poured himself a generous measure of brandy and tossed it off in one gulp. He seemed about to pour another one, but instead he set down the glass sharply. The next moment his fist slammed into the wall in a punch that shook the room.

He stayed motionless for a moment, then leaned his forehead against the wall as though his strength had drained away. Briony stared, horrified. He looked like a man in the extremity of agony.

Slowly she moved closer and touched him on the shoulder. He turned and stared at her with eyes that saw nothing. He was breathing heavily.

"Come and sit down," she said gently.

He let him draw her to the sofa, where he sat. He seemed only half aware of what he was doing.

"Your hand's bleeding," Briony said, examining the grazed and bruised knuckle. "Shall I call Nora—?"

"No," he said quickly. "I don't want her to see me like this." He took out a handkerchief and wound it round the hand. "Just pour me another brandy. A large one."

She did so and set it beside him. "What's the matter with Emma?" she asked quietly.

But her worst fears told her the answer even before he raised his head and said bleakly, "She's dying."

CHAPTER THREE

"SHE's dying," Carlyle repeated when Briony was silent.

Briony had half expected to hear something of the kind, but she had to brace herself against the blunt words before she could speak.

"She told me she'd been ill, but she spoke as if it was in the past—"

"She thinks it is, and she must go on thinking so. But it's not over. It won't be over until—" He stopped and shuddered. "It'll never be over," he finished.

"But—why?"

"Her heart. Her mother's heart wasn't strong. We didn't know that when we married, but late in the pregnancy she had a heart attack. We'd never dreamed—she seemed so strong—she survived the heart attack, but the doctor warned us that the birth would probably be too much for her. For the last month, we knew what was going to happen. We pretended we didn't, but we did. She had a Caesarean birth, to ease the strain on her but—" Carlyle couldn't go on. He raised both hands in a gesture of helplessness, and some powerful protective instinct made Briony enfold them in hers. He began to talk again. "She lived long enough to hold Emma in her arms. Then she fell into a coma. I stayed with her for two days, holding her hand, talking to her, but she never woke again."

Suddenly he seemed to notice that he was holding Briony's hands. He released her self-consciously, and made a visible effort to pull himself together. "I'm sorry.

I had no right to lose control and put you through it, too. Usually I manage things better.''

It would have been impossible for Briony to tell him that he was more likable now than the super-controlled man she saw at work. ''It's all right,'' she said gently. ''Just tell me whatever you want to.''

''The doctors warned me that Emma might have the same trouble as her mother, but for years I thought we'd got away with it. And then—suddenly—''

''But isn't there anything they can do?'' Briony asked. ''There are marvelous heart operations these days. Surely there's one for her?''

''Yes, if she were strong enough. But it's too late. She's too weak to stand the strain. It would simply mean her dying now instead of—in a few months.''

He looked at her. ''Do you understand? I'm trying to cram everything into those months. I'm trying to be the father I never made time to be before. I've always loved her, but building the firm up has taken a lot of my attention and—God forgive me, I thought she was all right.'' The words were a cry.

''Oh, heavens!'' Briony whispered, full of horror.

''I meant to be a better father than I've been, but I believed there was plenty of time. Do you know what she wants most in the world?''

''You?''

''No, a mother. That's all she's ever really wanted, to have a mother like other little girls. I always promised to get her one, but now I've left it too late. All I can do is try to give her everything else in the short time she has left.''

He drank his brandy and began talking again in a confused, desperate way. ''She pleaded to go to the funfair. I shouldn't have agreed—it was bound to be too much for her—but she wanted it so much—so I gave in. And then when she collapsed—how could I have been such a fool?''

''But she's not dying now?'' Briony asked quickly.

''No, the doctor says she just needs a good rest. But it's taken some of her strength, and she has so little left. How can I be sure if I did the right thing?'' He dropped his head into his hands.

Briony's heart ached for him. She knew only too well the agonies of self-reproach and regret that he was suffering. Hardly conscious of her actions, she gently took hold of his shoulders. After a moment he looked up and met her eyes. His face was ravaged.

''Listen to me,'' she said softly. ''You can't ever be totally sure you did the right thing. Life just doesn't make it easy for us like that. But if you love her, and she knows it, then—then that has to be enough. You mustn't torment yourself with guilt, because—'' Her voice shook. ''Because useless guilt is so destructive. You can only give her all your love and do what seems best at the time.''

His gaze was fixed on her, his attention caught by her tone and by a look of strain on her face that echoed his own.

''You understand, don't you?'' he said quietly.

''Yes, I understand.''

''Then it's easier for me to ask you to do something—not for me, but for Emma. She likes you. I've never seen her take to someone so quickly.''

''What do you want me to do?'' she asked with a heart full of dread.

''Be her friend until—for as long as she needs one. Let us spend some time with you. Let her pretend that you're her mother.''

She was backing away before the words were out. "No, I'm sorry. I can't do that."

"I know it's a lot to ask, but you like her, too, don't you?"

"Yes," Briony choked. "Too much."

"Please, it'll mean so much to her. And it won't be for long. Can't you see that?"

"Yes, I can. That's just what—I'm sorry, it's impossible."

"*Why?*" He stood and confronted her. "Are you afraid it'll take up too much time? I'll pay you anything you ask. You're relieved of all duties at the office, and I'll write you a blank paycheck, but you have to do this."

"I don't have to," she said passionately. "I don't want your money. If I could do it, I would, but I *can't*. It's you she needs, not me. I can't be more to her than her father."

"But she sees you as a mother figure, and that means that you are," he said, very pale. "Maybe that's another measure of my failure, but I have to accept that it's true. Please do this, Briony."

She felt she would go mad if she endured any more. She began to gather her things together in a rush. "I'm sorry, I just can't. Please don't press me. It's impossible."

"Briony—" He seized her arm.

"*No,*" she cried. "Let me go. I—I can't stay here."

He made no move to release her and she wrenched herself free. She had a last vision of his distraught face before she fled. The front door banged behind her and she was running down the long drive, into the street. She had no idea where she was but she ran without stopping until she reached an underground station.

Her journey took half an hour, and for all that time she kept herself in a state of frozen control. It lasted until she was home with her own front door safely shut behind her. As she went to put her doorkey away she saw the little whale in her bag, where she'd thrust it for safety. Somehow it was that sight that broke her, and she buried her face against the furry creature and sobbed helplessly. *Oh, Sally! Sally!*

She slept badly that night. When she managed to doze off she was tormented by dreams of Emma collapsing into her father's arms. Then Carlyle would turn to Briony, holding out his daughter, saying, "She's dying." Briony would wake with a start, splash cold water on her face and resolve not to doze again.

Lying awake was almost worse because she couldn't forget the moment when Carlyle had looked into her eyes; she'd seen his defenseless pain, and felt it as acutely as her own. Her heart had gone out to him and for a moment she'd been almost ready to do anything he asked. But only for a moment. Then she'd flinched away.

It wasn't only her memories of Sally that had made her back off. That afternoon she'd been touched by the compelling magnetism that surrounded Carlyle Brackman like an aura. Even when he was wandering through a funfair, thinking only of being a father, that magnetism had been there, filling the air with excitement. For Briony he was a dangerous man.

She had the poorest opinion of her own attractions. Although her figure was slender, it was the slenderness of an athlete rather than a model. Her shoulders were too square and, to her critical eyes, her whole body seemed angular.

She knew that her blond hair and blue eyes were good features, and if forced to consider her face she'd have said guardedly that it was "all right." But nothing could be more absurd than for her to fall under the spell of a man like Carlyle, who could attract any woman he wanted.

And she wouldn't allow it to happen, she assured herself. Just because their eyes had met and she'd felt she understood him as no other woman could, that didn't mean she had to walk into danger like someone hypnotized. She was a grown woman with a strong will of her own, and she would use that will to break the bond that threatened to join her heart to his: a bond that existed only on her own side.

Suddenly her hands seemed to tingle with memory. Only a few hours ago he'd clasped them in his own, passionately communicating his agony. There'd been need in that touch, and a desperate reaching out for help. Something in her longed to reach out in return, offering him all the consolation in her passionate, protective nature. But common sense forced her back. Getting close to Carlyle Brackman would only cause her more pain, and she didn't feel as if she could face any more just now.

By morning her mind was made up. She would hand in her notice today and ask the agency to find her something else. Before leaving home she put the little whale into her bag so that Carlyle could give it to Emma.

She walked slowly to the bus stop, held back by a dead weight that lay on her will. She didn't want to go into the office, see Carlyle, and be forced to confront her demons again.

Jenny was there ahead of her. She glanced at the clock. "It's all right," she said. "He isn't here yet."

"At this hour?"

"I know. It's incredible, isn't it? Oh, Briony, I've got such news."

Her shining face told the whole story. "You and Michael have made up," Briony said.

"He came here yesterday afternoon, with just one red rose. It's so lucky Mr. Brackman was out because we had a long talk and everything's perfect again. We're getting married next month."

Briony's own pain eased. It was good to know that there was happiness in the world for nice people like Jenny. She listened to the whole story twice over, smiling and saying the proper things. But her mind's eye kept seeing Carlyle's suffering face.

At last Jenny said, "Hey, what happened after you all left yesterday?"

"We went to the funfair," Briony said.

"With Emma? Isn't she a darling? You know, it's a funny thing about that child. I've worked here for three years and until a few months ago I didn't even know he had a daughter. Then suddenly she started appearing in the office, and he'd always put work aside to take her out. She's pretty, isn't she? She's going to grow up a real beauty."

Briony made a noncommittal reply and tried to get on with her work, but she couldn't concentrate. She wondered if Carlyle's lateness meant that Emma had got worse. She knew how heartless her refusal to help must have seemed to him, but she couldn't face it. She'd spoken the truth when she said she liked Emma too much. It would be easy to love the mischievous child, whose frail health hadn't lessened her spirit. And Briony couldn't bear to love another little girl and see her die.

He came in midway through the morning, and strode straight to his office without looking at them. Almost at once the buzzer went on Briony's desk. "Come in here, please," he said over the intercom.

He looked as if he'd had a terrible night. There were dark shadows under his eyes and his face was drawn. She guessed that she looked as bad as he, because when he glanced up at her she saw something in his eyes— perhaps recognition, or fellow feeling— that made him grow still.

"How is Emma?" she asked at once.

"Well enough. I sat up with her most of the night, but she slept well. I've told Nora to make sure she stays in bed today."

"I'm sorry I can't do what you ask. In fact, I can't go on working for you, Mr. Brackman." She held out the whale. "I'd like you to give Emma this, and say goodbye to her for me."

He surveyed her out of hard eyes. "You really are abandoning us, aren't you?"

"You've no right to say that," she flashed. "I have good reasons."

"Are there any good reasons to turn your back on a sick child?"

She flinched but stood her ground. "You'll just have to believe that there are," she said.

He didn't answer in words but thrust a hand into his briefcase and brought out a pink envelope. "Emma's written you a letter," he said, holding it out to her. "Will you take it, or shall I tell her you threw it back at her?"

"That's blackmail," Briony flashed angrily.

He shrugged. "My daughter's dying and I'll be as unscrupulous as I have to be to get her what she wants."

She almost snatched it from him. The envelope contained a crayoned picture of herself, Carlyle and Emma at the fair. Underneath Emma had scribbled "Please come to tea with me."

Conscious of Carlyle's sharp eyes on her, Briony struggled with herself for a long moment before saying, "All right. Just this once. You can tell Emma I'll be glad to have tea with her."

"Thank you," he said. "It'll mean the world to her."

"As soon as she's better I'll visit her and—"

"Why not just come home with me this afternoon?"

"All right. This afternoon. This one time. After that—"

"We can discuss it on the way home," he said. "Now, can we get on with some work?"

Once that would have sounded like the heartless robot she'd called him, but she knew Carlyle Brackman better now. It shamed her to think how only yesterday she'd said that he could have no personal life and therefore no personal problems. The truth was that he was a proud, sensitive man who kept his agony hidden from the world because he couldn't bear to share it. Only by accident had she been granted a glimpse of his breaking heart. He didn't like that. His manner told her so. He'd invited her back in for Emma's sake, but it galled him that she'd seen his wounds. It would be better for both of them when she'd gone.

In the early afternoon he looked out of his office and nodded to her without speaking. As they walked to the car he said, "I called home and told Emma you were coming. She's thrilled."

Briony said nothing. She had a feeling of being drawn in against her will. But she wasn't going to let it happen. As he maneuvered the car into the stream of traffic she resolved to tell Carlyle about Sally. She'd flinched from speaking of it before, but it was better for him to understand her reasons.

"I'm sorry about the way I just ran off yesterday," she began.

"That's all right. I was only concerned about you getting home. If you'd waited, Tom would have driven you."

"I got home all right, thank you. But what I wanted to say—"

"Just a minute. There's something blocking me up ahead." He leaned out of the window and called to another driver. "That's better," he said, coming in again. "The traffic's always terrible on this road. What were you saying?"

"There's something I need to explain so that you—" She stopped as Carlyle swerved quickly down a side road, escaping a jam up ahead. "It had better wait," she said.

"Uh-huh!"

After about fifteen minutes they swung into a pleasant, tree-lined drive. Briony had had no attention for her surroundings the day before, but now she could see that Carlyle's large, detached house stood well back from the road, almost hidden by the trees in the garden. Like the car, it was quietly luxurious, the property of a man who'd made a fortune but didn't need to brag about it; or perhaps simply a man whose wealth meant nothing to him, because it couldn't save the one he loved.

As they got out he said, "What was it you were going to tell me? *Oh, no,* what's she doing there?"

Briony followed his pointing finger to a window overlooking the drive, where they could see Emma. "She's supposed to be in bed," Carlyle said. "She's not even in her room. She must have come into the hall to reach that window."

As they watched, Nora appeared, drawing Emma away from the window. Briony followed Carlyle up the wide staircase. Nora was just emerging from Emma's room. "I've made her get back in bed," she said. "Honestly, I did my best to stop her getting up—"

"All right, it's not your fault," Carlyle said. "I know what a handful she can be. Let's not keep her waiting." He opened the door of Emma's room. "Guess who's here," he said, standing aside to reveal Briony.

Until this moment Briony had promised herself to stay detached, but that was before she saw Emma, propped up by pillows in bed. At the sight of her the child's face broke into a beaming, joyous smile and she held out her arms in a gesture of wholehearted invitation and acceptance. The last of Briony's detachment fell away, and in another moment she ran across the floor to enfold Emma in a hug.

"I knew you'd come. I knew you'd come," Emma whispered in her ear. "Daddy said you wouldn't, but I knew you would."

"Of course I came," Briony said with an inward prayer of thanks that she'd been saved from disappointing this trusting child.

"We're all ready for you," Emma declared.

"We?"

"Oswald said he *had* to come to tea, as well, so I let him."

A small table, laid out for tea, had been set up by the bed. Oswald was perched on a chair, surveying the feast. Inspired, Briony plunged into her bag. "Look who else insisted on coming," she said, producing the little whale.

Emma beamed, clearly taking this for evidence that they were on the same wavelength. "You brought him," she squealed. "You *knew*."

"Yes, I suppose I must have known," Briony said guardedly. She was intensely conscious of Carlyle's cool eyes on her. He knew she hadn't brought the toy to work to please Emma. The little's girl's insistence on ascribing the best motives to her was painful.

"We've got tea and toast, and honey," Emma said, like a good hostess.

"That's good." Briony settled the whale in the crook of the penguin's flipper. "Because Oswald likes honey. Shall I pour?"

"Yes, please. Daddy has his tea without sugar."

"Oh, am I invited, too?" Carlyle enquired. "I thought it was just for you two, plus Oswald and Oswald."

Emma giggled, and Briony looked at Carlyle with new respect. It wasn't much of a joke, but it was a good effort from a man whose heart was breaking. Her respect for him increased even more when he sat down and joined in the tea party with every sign of enjoyment. Emma was in seventh heaven and it was clear her father's presence had put the seal on her pleasure.

"Do you like my room?" Emma asked her.

It was an enchanting room for a child, large and airy, with pale-colored decor and furnishings, and a huge window that looked out onto the garden. On the bedside table stood a large photograph of a young woman whose startling resemblance to Emma left no doubt that this was her mother. The walls were covered in pictures of ballerinas, and a pair of ballet shoes hung over the bed.

"I'm going to be a dancer," Emma confided. "When I'm older, Daddy says I can go to ballet school."

"That's right, darling," Carlyle agreed. "In a couple of years."

"Oh, sooner, Daddy, please."

"Well, maybe one year. When you're stronger."

She pouted. "You're always saying that. I wish it was next year now."

"I don't," Carlyle said involuntarily. Then he checked himself and added, "I just don't want you to grow up too fast."

"I want to grow up ever so fast. I want it to be next year, and the year after and the year after—"

"I think Oswald wants some more tea," Briony said quickly, seeing the strain on Carlyle's face. How much of this could he take? she wondered.

Nora put her head round the door. "Telephone for you," she said.

Carlyle kissed his daughter and left, promising to be back soon. Briony happened to be watching Emma as he left and saw her relax slightly as soon as he'd gone, in a manner that uncannily echoed his own way of switching a cheerful face on and off for her.

Oh, no, she thought. She can't really have any idea. It's impossible. I'm imagining things.

She saw Emma trying to plump up the pillows and went to help her. "Is that better?" she said when she'd finished.

"Yes, thank you." Emma lay back and Briony's arm went out instinctively to draw her in so that the child was lying in its curve. This was how Sally had often lain, but Briony refused to let the memory of that hurt her now. She felt ashamed of the way she'd tried to avoid Emma.

How could I do it, when she needs me so much? she thought. As though anything mattered but helping her.

"Do you ever go to the ballet?" Emma asked.

"Yes, I love ballet."

"Will you take me, one day?"

"Of course I will. What shall we go and see?"

"Well, my favorite is *The Sleeping Beauty*, but I like *Giselle* too—"

Briony let her ramble happily through her thoughts, now and then putting in a word of encouragement. Emma seemed to need not so much conversation as her physical presence to snuggle against. Gradually her voice slowed and her head began to droop as weariness overtook her again. At last there was silence.

There was a click of the door as Carlyle entered. When he saw Emma motionless against Briony, a look of fear came into his face, but she put a finger to her lips and mouthed "Asleep."

He came quietly forward and looked at his daughter with an expression of such anguished love that Briony felt she should turn away. But she couldn't make herself do it. Carlyle's face was poignant as he gently brushed the hair back on Emma's forehead.

"Let's settle her," Briony whispered.

She eased Emma down in the bed, removed the extra pillows and drew the cover up. Emma seemed fast asleep, but she murmured something.

"I didn't catch that," Briony said. "What was it?"

"She asked for Oswald," Carlyle said in a voice that sounded faintly husky. He put the penguin into bed beside her.

"No, *Oswald*," Emma whispered.

Understanding now, he added the whale, and Emma's blissful smile told him he'd got it right.

"Good night darling," Briony said, kissing her, and felt an arm go around her neck. She walked out quickly, leaving Carlyle alone with his daughter.

Downstairs she took deep breaths to steady herself, and was calm by the time he joined her in the front room. From the look on his face she guessed that he, too, had had to fight for control.

"You know you can't abandon her now, don't you?" he said.

"Yes, I know."

"Emma needs you."

"Yes. I'll come to see her—"

"That's not good enough. You handed in your notice this morning—"

"I'll take it back."

"And give it in again whenever you like. Besides, I don't need you in the office, I need you here, loving her, and letting her love you. That's what she wants to do more than anything."

"I'll be here—"

"Living here. Night and day."

"Are you offering me another job as a child minder?"

"No, I'm asking you to marry me," he said simply.

She stared in outrage. "That has to be the unfunniest joke of all time."

"Joke? Do you think I'd make a joke about this?"

"Then if it's not a joke—"

"I told you, Emma wants a mother. She's never known what it was like to have one, and I want to give her this before she dies. She's set her heart on you."

"But—" She pressed her hands to her head as if to hold her whirling thoughts in check.

"Is there someone else?" he demanded. "A boyfriend, fiancé, lover—whatever?"

"No, there's no one else."

"So there's nothing to stop you pretending to be my wife for a few months. That's all it would be, a pretense. I won't ask anything of you for myself. When it's over you can have a divorce with any settlement you like. You need never work again. Or if you want to work, you can come into the company and with your brains you'll rise to the top. All I ask is that you give Emma a few months, so that she doesn't die without ever knowing what it is to have a mother.''

"I can't take this in,'' she said desperately.

"Emma's had everything that money could buy, but I know now that she's never had the things that really matter.'' He took a shuddering breath. ''I don't want her to lose out on this, as well. Please, Briony. *Please.*''

His voice was desperate. His eyes looked as she'd seen them once before, anguished and defenseless, and she was filled with a sense of danger. To marry him, to live close to him for months, when her heart was coming painfully alive to him. To do this, knowing that in the end she must leave him. It would be madness.

Then she thought of the child upstairs, putting on a smiling face for her father, being stronger and braver than any child should have to be, asking only this one thing from all the many things life had denied her.

"All right,'' she said steadily to Carlyle. ''I'll marry you, for her sake.''

She didn't know what sort of reaction to expect from him, but when it came it took her by surprise. Instead of words, he raised her hand and laid it against his lips. It wasn't a flirtatious gesture, but one of reverence.

"Thank you,'' he said softly.

The touch of his lips unnerved her, reminding her how hard this marriage was going to be in some ways. She disengaged her hand, not looking at him.

"By the way,'' he said, ''what was it you wanted to tell me?''

"What?''

"You said there was something you had to explain, about why you didn't want to be with Emma. Was it important?"

"No," she said. "It wasn't important at all."

CHAPTER FOUR

BRIONY left the firm the next day and began spending her time with Emma. It was four days before they felt the child was strong enough for the excitement of being told the news. During that time Carlyle booked the register office for three weeks ahead.

Emma turned to Briony more and more. She liked nothing better than to have her read her to sleep, and often she would doze off holding her hand. It was clear that whatever Carlyle decided, Emma had already made her choice.

Once Emma found her studying the picture by her bed. "That was my Mummy," she confided. "She died when I was a baby."

The picture showed a young woman with a delicate, ethereal beauty. A man could hardly help falling in love with her, thought Briony. "She was really enchanting," she said with an unconscious little sigh.

"Enchanting," Emma repeated. She reached for a notebook and pencil by the bed, and looked up expectantly. Briony spelled "enchanting" and Emma wrote it down, frowning as she concentrated.

"I like new words," she said. "They're fun."

"What a good idea. Your own private dictionary."

"Dictionary," said Emma at once.

Briony spelled this, too. While Emma wrote, she studied the picture, envying Helen Brackman her grace and charm.

"Daddy says she was prettier than anyone in the world," Emma said.

"Yes, she was. And you're so like her."

Emma was pleased. "Yes, Daddy says so, too. He's always telling me how much I look like her."

And losing Emma would be like losing his wife all over again, Briony thought. She caught Emma watching her, and smiled quickly.

One evening, as she and Carlyle were tucking Emma into bed, she asked casually, "We've had good times together these last few days, haven't we?"

Emma nodded. "I wish you could stay forever," she said wistfully.

"Would you really like me to do that?" Briony asked, relieved that Emma had prepared the way.

"Oo-oh, yes."

"All right, then. I will."

"We're going to get married," Carlyle said from the other side of the bed.

Emma looked from one to the other as if in disbelief. Then joy flooded her face and she jumped up in bed to throw her arms around Briony's neck. "Really? Really?"

"Yes, really," she laughed, trying to keep from strangling.

"Hey, what about me?" Carlyle asked with a grin. "Don't I get a hug?"

Emma put her arms around him. "Is it really true?" she begged.

"Really true," Briony confirmed, touched by the child's joy. It felt so good to be wanted.

"When did it happen?" Emma asked. "I mean, when did you ask Briony?"

"A few days ago," Carlyle said. "We were waiting for the right moment to tell you."

"But where did you propose? Was it in the office, or here, or—it was at the funfair, wasn't it?"

"Sort of," Carlyle said lamely.

"Oh, please tell me about it."

"We can't," Briony said, coming to his rescue. "Things like that have to stay a secret."

Emma seemed to understand this because she sat back, apparently satisfied. But the next moment she caught them off guard again, seizing Briony's left hand, which was conspicuously bare. "Daddy hasn't bought you a ring yet," she said in tones of disappointment.

"That's going to come next," Carlyle said hastily.

"When we've got time," Briony put in. "I wanted to spend these past few days with you so that we could get to know each other."

"You will get married *soon*, won't you?" Emma asked eagerly.

"Very soon," Carlyle promised her. "In fact, before the end of this month."

"And can I be a bridesmaid?"

"But, darling—" Briony began awkwardly.

"Your *chief* bridesmaid, with a pink satin dress?" Emma went on ecstatically. "And you'll have a huge bouquet of white roses, and when you get to the altar you'll hand it to me to look after for you. Oh, do say yes."

Briony looked at Carlyle, nonplussed. Neither of them had anticipated this situation, but he was equal to it. "Of course you can," he said. "Whatever you like."

"No, Briony has to say so," Emma told her father severely. "She's the bride."

"I think your idea sounds absolutely wonderful," she said warmly.

"Can I help you choose your wedding dress?"

"As soon as you're well enough to get up, we'll go to the hire shop."

"Hire?" Emma looked scandalized. "Aren't you going to buy one?"

"There's no need. I'll only wear it once—"

"But don't you want to keep it for years and years, and look at it when you grow old?" Emma asked anxiously.

It was clear that her vision of a perfect wedding included this epilogue. Briony was briefly nonplussed, but Carlyle said, "Of course we'll buy it to keep, and you'll help Briony choose it. That's much better."

He kissed his daughter and left the room with Briony. Downstairs they faced each other awkwardly. "I never dreamed of anything like this," he admitted. "I thought if I gave her a mother everything would be all right. But she's set her heart on something more."

"She wants to feel herself as part of a family," Briony said, "doing what families do."

"It's not going to be the quiet ceremony we planned. Can you endure a big church wedding, with all the frills?"

"If it's what makes Emma happy." Briony gave a faint smile. "I'll have to take my directions from her. Let's just hope she doesn't want to buy up the whole shop."

He shrugged. "What does it matter if she does? Get whatever she wants. Find a good wedding organizer to plan everything and tell them to send the bills to me. I'll give you my credit card so that you can buy an engagement ring. What's the matter? Why are you looking at me like that?"

"Don't you realize it's not so simple anymore? Emma's got very fixed ideas about how things should happen."

"And how does she want this to happen?"

"I think you should ask Emma's advice about the ring and, if possible, take it. That will please her more than anything."

"Take her advice," he repeated as if memorizing a lesson.

"Make a conspiracy of it. Just you and her."

"Right. Yes. That's good."

She regarded him with a mixture of pity, kindness and exasperation. He knew all about business, but people had to be explained to him, even those he loved. But when Carlyle undertook any task he did it well, and the following evening he brought home a large jeweler's box, which he took straight to Emma's room. Briony found herself firmly excluded, but from behind the door she could hear Emma giggling and saying, "That one—no that one."

At last Emma looked out. "You can come in now," she said, taking Briony's hand. She drew her into the room where Carlyle was waiting with something hidden in his hand. "Do I have to go away?" she asked anxiously.

"Of course not," Briony said at once. "This is a family occasion."

She felt self-conscious taking part in what should have been a romantic moment, and she wondered if Carlyle felt the same. But he seemed composed as he held out his hand to take hers, and said, "Emma and I chose this together. She's convinced it's the one you'll like, and I hope you do."

Briony almost gasped when she saw the ring. With cheerful disregard for her father's pocket Emma had picked a glittering confection of diamonds. There must have been thirty tiny stones clustered around one larger one in the center.

"Do you like it?" Emma asked eagerly.

"It's beautiful," Briony breathed as Carlyle slid the ring onto her left hand. She smiled at Emma. "You made a lovely choice."

"Daddy helped," she said generously. She gave her father a significant look and whispered loudly, "Go *on*, Daddy."

For a moment Briony didn't understand. Emma was regarding her father anxiously, as though fearful that he'd omit something and spoil the moment. Then Briony felt Carlyle's hands on her shoulders and he was drawing her near. The next moment his lips were on hers.

There was nothing passionate about the kiss. It was a formality for Emma's sake. But the touch of his mouth caught Briony unaware and a response awoke deep inside her before she could guard against it. She stood there, stunned, until he murmured against her lips, "Kiss me back or it won't look right."

She hastened to play her part, laying her hands on his arms and leaning closer. His mouth was firm and warm against hers, and suddenly images began to chase through her mind: hot summer days full of sweet, languorous beauty; the earth in bloom; crimson sunsets and scented breezes; wine and laughter and love. Suddenly she was achingly aware of a world full of possibilities, and all because of a light kiss from a man who cared nothing for her and expected her to care nothing for him.

They drew apart, and Briony quickly turned her head. Her heart was beating rapidly, and she was sure that her face was flushed. "It's a beautiful ring," she said, trying to speak calmly. "I'll treasure it."

When they were alone a few minutes later Carlyle said awkwardly, "I'm really sorry about that. I never meant it to happen. It didn't occur to me that she'd get so involved with the details.''

"Nor me. It doesn't matter," she said hastily.

"I'll make sure it happens as little as possible. I promise you I've no wish to—well, I'm sure you feel the same—"

"Exactly," she said. "Let's drop the subject, shall we?"

She went home early that evening, refusing to let Carlyle or Tom drive her. She wanted to be alone to come to terms with the dismaying thing that had happened to her. Her heart and her senses had been insistently warming to Carlyle despite her resolutions. But she felt she could have coped, if only she could keep him at arm's length. It seemed that was to be denied her. The lightest touch of his lips had affected her so strongly that it was as if the solid ground had vanished from beneath her, revealing that she was actually walking a tightrope across a chasm.

How could she live close to this man for months without responding to him, loving him? Her heart told her that it wasn't possible. Yet she must find a way if she was to do what she'd promised.

Then Emma's face came into her mind, shining, trustful. If she tried hard she could put Carlyle's image aside, and think only of the little girl who needed her.

The ring caught her eye, its glittering beauty seeming to mock her. A woman who'd been given such a ring for love would treasure it and never take it off for a moment. But this was a stage prop, to be returned when the show was over. Before she went to bed she put it carefully away in a drawer.

*   *   *

Briony dreaded shopping for a dress with Emma, but when the day arrived she found the child's enthusiasm infectious. Nora came, too, to care for Emma while Briony was occupied in the changing room, and the three of them went into central London, to the bridal department of a store so expensive that in the past Briony had always hurried past its doors. Now she was an honored customer with a limitless budget.

Confronted with a range of pink satin dresses, Emma was rendered speechless with joy for a full ten seconds before plunging in. In fact she managed to find what she wanted in the first few minutes, trying it on and immediately announcing, "This one."

She was far more choosy about the bride's gown, airily discarding several that Briony felt would have done very well. It was clear that she had a vision in her mind, and nothing would do for her but to fulfill it. Briony was apprehensive about the outcome. She looked best in uncluttered lines, and she was afraid the child would pick one of the fairy-tale fantasies, covered in ribbons and frills, that was on display.

At last Emma pointed to a gown and suggested, "Try this."

As soon as she saw herself in it Briony knew Emma's taste was unerring. The dress was made of heavy silk, high in the neck, shaped to the waist then falling over her hips in a very slight flare and dropping straight to the floor. The back stretched out in a long train and the sleeves grew wider as they descended, until they almost touched the pale gray carpet. The only decoration was a sprinkling of seed pearls.

"I've never felt silk as heavy as this," she murmured.

"It's specially woven for this shop, madam," said the assistant, "to give it the extra weight. Try walking in it."

Briony took a few steps and the dress flowed out behind her, a thing of glorious beauty. As if by magic it seemed to correct all the imperfections of her body. square shoulders ceased to be noticeable, and her angular appearance vanished, replaced by a soft, feminine roundness that she had never believed could be hers. She was awed, and felt quite unequal to wearing it. Despite its simplicity this gown had a magnificence that contrasted with the way she saw herself: down-to-earth, reliable, perhaps even a little prosaic.

"I don't think—" she began.

"Oh, but you must," Emma said eagerly. "And look, here's the perfect veil to go with it."

The veil was equally overwhelming, stretching down almost the full length of the train. It framed Briony's face in a cloud of soft white that made her skin glow and her eyes look huge. She began to walk again, and Emma fell into step behind her, holding up the train as they paraded down the long, mirrored room.

"She's right," Nora said. "You look marvelous."

"How much is this dress?" Briony asked. The assistant told her. "*How* much?" she gasped. "Oh, goodness, it's far too—"

"We'll take it," Emma said calmly. And the deed was done.

"She just overrode me like a juggernaut," Briony told Carlyle defensively that night. "Remember that when you get the bill."

"I know her in her juggernaut moods," Carlyle observed. He grinned suddenly. "I can't think where she gets it from."

They were having supper in her little flat. Now that Briony was spending her days with Emma this was their one chance to talk. The time was slipping away fast, making her feel caught up in a whirlwind. Very soon she would become the wife of this man, at least in name. She felt powerfully attracted to him, yet he was still essentially a stranger, and he discussed their wedding as he would have done any other arrangement that he expected to be handled efficiently. It made it hard for her to broach a subject she knew she couldn't delay any longer.

"Is everything going all right?" he asked now.

"Mrs. Grainger has everything in hand," she said, naming the wedding organizer. "Considering the short time we've given her, she's done a marvelous job."

"Then what's on your mind? Emma's happy, isn't she?"

"Perfectly. She's full of plans for us—" Briony stopped awkwardly.

"What pitfall has she opened at our feet now?" he asked warily. "Go on, tell me the worst. I'm beginning to expect it." He looked suddenly horrified. "Oh, lord, don't tell me she wants us to have a honeymoon?"

"No, I got out of that by saying that we don't want to leave her, and she isn't well enough to go with us."

"Then what haven't we thought of?"

"Where I'm going to sleep."

"But we agreed that you'd have the room next to Emma."

"I know, but she's got it fixed in her head that your room has to be redecorated to make it suitable for me to share it. She told me on the way home today that she wants to help choose the new decor. It's all part of her mental picture of family life. She's stayed overnight with her friends, so she knows married people share a room. She told me so."

He looked alarmed. "What did you say?"

"I referred her to you," Briony said firmly.

"Well, I suppose—if she's set her heart—"

"*No,*" Briony said quickly. "I will not share a room with you. That wasn't in our agreement. You'll just have to tell her—I don't know—say I want to be close to her in case she's ill in the night."

"That will sound too suspicious. She thinks she's getting better. I don't want any risk that she might guess the truth."

Briony was silent and thoughtful for a long moment before asking, "Hasn't it ever crossed your mind that she might have guessed already?"

"Of course not," he said a little too quickly.

"Carlyle," she said gently, "you can't tell how much Emma knows."

"She doesn't know anything," he said brusquely. "I've made sure of it."

"You can't 'make sure of it.' You don't know what's going on in her mind. She's very bright and perceptive."

He looked at her coldly, and his tone was suddenly arctic. "I tell you it's impossible!" he said in a deliberate voice. "She thinks she's recovering, and I intend her to go on thinking that way."

"I hope you're right," Briony said patiently. "But you *might* be wrong. I've seen the way she consciously brightens up when you come into the room. You're putting on a show to reassure her, but I think she's doing the same for you."

His face was hard, closed against her. "Rubbish! Good God, what can you know about her in such a short time?"

The injustice of this made her temper flare. "You evidently felt I was good at getting close to her or we wouldn't be having this discussion."

"I asked you in to help Emma, not spout a lot of fanciful theories—"

"And I think I help her best by understanding her. What about when you were considering an operation? Didn't she know about that?"

"Yes, but I dealt with it. I told her she didn't need an operation, that everything would be all right as long as she was careful."

"But don't you realize that Emma knows what she *knows*, not just what she's told?"

"I tell you she has no idea of the truth," Carlyle shouted. "She believes what I tell her. I want Emma's last few months to be perfect for her, and I asked you to help me make them perfect, *not to interfere.*"

Briony stared at him, shocked by the explosion she'd touched off. She knew it was pain that made Carlyle so unreasonable, pain that his dream of giving Emma the perfect happiness he'd never given her before might be unattainable. She could feel compassion for that pain, but she wasn't going to let him walk over her like this.

"Is it interfering to disagree with you?" she demanded crossly.

"Do you know what you're saying?" he demanded, his face livid. "You're saying it's too late to make her happy—"

"I'm not—"

"Don't you realize that her happiness is the *only* thing that counts with me? *Nothing and nobody else matters.* I'll do anything to make her last few months perfect—"

"But you'll do that best by understanding what she wants," Briony said. "Can't you see how wrong you've been about everything? Emma doesn't just want a mother, she wants a complete family because she's never known that kind of total security.''

"She's always known that I love her—"

"But how much of your attention has she had? You thought you had years to be the perfect father, but now there aren't any years, you're trying to give her a whole childhood in a few months. But who are you doing it for, Carlyle? Her or yourself?''

She hadn't meant to say so much, but the words had poured out. She hated herself for hurting a man already wounded, yet for his child's sake there were things he needed to face.

But it was too late. She knew that when she saw the look he turned on her. "That's enough!" he snapped. "I won't have you ruining her last months with your idiot theories.'' He took a deep breath. "Cancel everything. From now on you stay right away from her.''

She stared. "You're calling it off?"

"Exactly. She's better off without you."

"But you'll break her heart," Briony cried. "You can't do this to her. It's cruel.''

"Not half as cruel as the damage you could do her. You'd better let me have the ring before we forget it.''

He held out his hand. Moving as in a trance Briony handed him the ring. She couldn't believe what was happening. While she was still trying to take it in, Carlyle flung her one final look of hate, then walked out of her flat, and she heard his footsteps growing fainter.

It took Briony a long time to get to sleep, and when she did doze off, Emma was there, looking at her sadly. She cried out, but Emma vanished and the world was suddenly full of a loud, persistent ringing. She woke to the realization that someone was pressing her doorbell.

The clock said five in the morning. She stumbled out of bed and pulled on a light dressing gown over her cotton nightdress. The bell was still ringing as she went sleepily into the hall and switched on the light which, mercifully, had the effect of making whoever was out there take their finger off the bell. She opened the door to find Carlyle.

He looked terrible. There were dark shadows under his eyes and he seemed like a man who'd been through hell. He was still wearing the clothes he'd worn when he'd stormed out, but in contrast to his immaculate appearance then, the throat of his shirt had been torn open and his tie hung awry.

"May I come in?" he asked.

She stood back for him to pass, and closed the front door. In her front room he turned to face her. "Is it too late to ask for your forgiveness?" he said quietly.

She forgave him at once. Wretchedness was written all over his face, and she couldn't bear it. "It's all right," she said.

"No!" He shook his head as though trying to clear his mind. "It's not all right. I had no business speaking to you like that just because you told me—things I didn't want to hear."

"I'm probably wrong," she said quickly.

"No—yes—I don't know. But I wouldn't even listen to you because if you're right—" It seemed as if he had to force the next words out. "You see, I wanted everything to be perfect for her. But it's too late, isn't it?" His face was haggard.

A thousand words sprang to Briony's lips, but she dismissed them all. Words were useless now. She put out her arms and he went blindly into them. *"Help me,"* he whispered.

He held her tightly, desperately, as though she was the only refuge in a hideous world. Briony was filled with a sensation that was half anguish, half delight. It felt so right to hold him, offering the warmth and comfort that he needed so badly. She stroked his untidy hair and rested her cheek against his.

"I'm sorry for what I said," she murmured. "I didn't mean it all to come out like that—"

"But it's true, isn't it?" he said with self-condemning bitterness. "I'm doing it for myself, to ease my own conscience about not being a better father sooner. But I swear to you I'd give my own life for Emma. She's the only person in the world I love—"

"I know," Briony said with a little sigh. "I know."

He drew back to look at her. "I don't know what to do," he confessed. "I'm floundering around, trying to do the right thing, and always getting it wrong, because in the end there *is* no right thing. In the end she's going to die, and I'm trying to pretend it's not true." His eyes were bleak and terrible. "But it *is* true, isn't it?"

"Yes," she said. "It's true."

Then, because there was nothing else to do, she laid her mouth gently on his for a moment. He didn't kiss her back, but he accepted her kiss, and she felt his big, strong body relax in her arms. When he took his lips from hers, he didn't draw away, but let his head rest on her shoulder as though too weary to do anything but seek comfort.

At last she forced herself to let him go. To be this close to him was dangerous. She wanted too much, but he wasn't interested in her as a woman. "Let me make you some coffee," she said with an attempt at lightness. She straightened his tie. "You need looking after."

He followed her into the kitchen. "I haven't been home since I left here," he said. "I drove for a while. Then I got out and walked for miles—God knows where—anywhere—"

"You look exhausted."

"I wanted to be too tired to think. But it didn't work. I couldn't get away from what was really driving me, the knowledge that you may be right. That's why I was so angry with you."

She nodded and set his coffee before him. He hesitated before saying, "Could you bear to take us on again, Emma and me? It won't be easy."

"I'll manage." She smiled at him. "You need me. Both of you."

"Yes, we do."

"But, Carlyle, if I'm going to be Emma's mother, then you must let me be her *mother*. A real mother, not someone who can be reduced to the hired help whenever it suits you."

He winced, but accepted it. "It won't happen again," he promised. "I trust you better than I trust myself." He gave a half smile. "I think I instinctively knew that about you from the start—that you could be trusted."

"From the start?" she queried lightly. "You mean, those two months when you didn't notice I was there?"

"No, I mean the day I did notice you—was it only three weeks ago?—when you handled the worst I could throw at you without making any notes, and never got a thing wrong. I knew then you were efficient and reliable. I never guessed how important those qualities were to become to me."

Old reliable, she thought wryly. *That's how he sees me.* But at least he needed her. She could take comfort in that.

"What would I do if I hadn't found you?" he mused aloud.

"It doesn't matter. You did find me, and I'm here for you."

"You're a most forgiving woman—"

"I said terrible things too," she said quickly.

"I don't just mean that. I promised I wouldn't make any demands on you, but I quarrel with you, and bully you—"

"I can stand up for myself."

He managed the ghost of a smile. "Well, I guess I know that now."

He took the diamond ring from his pocket and put it on her finger. He didn't speak, but for a moment his hand gripped hers tightly.

"I'd better be off home," he said huskily. "Good night. And thank you."

CHAPTER FIVE

In the end, Briony lost the battle to have her own room. Carlyle conceded, but Emma outmaneuvered them both.

"It's a wedding present to both of you, from me," she explained, indicating a huge box from the same store where Briony had bought her wedding dress. It had been delivered earlier in the day, but Emma had refused to let Briony look inside until her father was there, too.

Together they opened the box and discovered a huge, luxurious bedspread, created from silk patchwork, cunningly designed to suggest a jungle. It was a work of art and at any other time Briony would have rejoiced in its beauty. Now all she saw was that she'd been comprehensively defeated.

"Let's put it on, and see how it looks," Emma begged. She tugged at Briony's hand.

"You go on ahead of us," Carlyle said, turning away to hide the fact that his lips were twitching. When they were alone he gave her a pleading look. Briony met his eyes defiantly, until at last her lips, too, began to quiver. At the same moment they both began to laugh.

"I swear I didn't put her up to this," he said.

"I wouldn't put anything past you."

"You do me an injustice. My mind isn't nearly as subtle and convoluted as Emma's."

"Well, what do we do now?" she demanded.

"My instinct is simply to give in, but I know you'll think that shockingly spineless."

She sighed. "Oh, well—"

"You'll never regret it, Briony, I promise."

"I'm regretting it already," she said with a laugh.

"Come *on*," Emma yelled down through the banisters.

"Coming, coming," they said, hoisting the bedspread between them and making their way obediently upstairs.

With a week to go, Carlyle's mother moved into the house. Briony was apprehensive before they met, and even more so when she discovered that Joyce Brackman had sharp eyes that seemed to see everything.

"How much have you told her?" she asked Carlyle.

"She knows I'm marrying for Emma's sake," he admitted, "but I haven't said anything about our bargain."

Joyce was inclined to regard Briony askance until she saw that Emma loved her. After that her reserve melted and Briony soon discovered that a warm heart underlay Joyce's shrewdness. It was she who, after a visit to Briony's little flat, suggested that she should be married from Carlyle's house.

"You need to make a grand entrance in that dress," she said. "And you can't make a grand entrance down seven floors of a tower block. Besides, if you've got no family you'll need me there to help you. You did say you had no family, didn't you?"

"That's right," Briony said quietly. She was thinking of how this wedding might have been with Sally sharing bridesmaid duties with Emma. How lovely they would have looked, walking side-by-side down the aisle, identically dressed in pink satin—

But there the vision collapsed. The tomboyish Sally might have worn pink satin for Briony's sake, but no power on earth would have made her comfortable in it. She'd have fiddled and scratched until she could rid herself of the hated dress with a sigh of relief. For a moment the picture was so clear that Briony smiled in affectionate amusement. It was the first time she'd remembered Sally with more pleasure than pain.

Then she came back to the present, to discover Carlyle and Joyce regarding her with puzzled looks.

"What is it, dear?" Joyce asked. "You went off into a dream."

"Nothing," Briony said hastily. "I think your idea of being married from here is lovely."

The day before the wedding the house began to fill up with cousins and aunts. Emma rapidly grew beside herself with excitement, and soon after tea Briony declared that it was time for her to go to bed.

"Oh, not yet," Emma cried in dismay.

"You've got a big day tomorrow and you won't be up to it if you don't get a good night's sleep," Briony said firmly. She was really worried at the thought of Emma overdoing it.

"But I'm better now," Emma pleaded. "I am. Really I am."

"I know. But you won't stay better if you get overtired," Briony said patiently. "Off to bed."

With comical suddenness Emma's face changed. The angelic fairy vanished, to be replaced by a mutinous child. "I *won't* get overtired," she said belligerently. "I'm not tired. I'm *not*."

"Emma, go to bed," Briony said with quiet firmness.

"But everybody's here. Oh, *please*, Mummy."

It was the first time she'd used the word. Briony smiled with pleasure, and Briony dropped down on one knee in front of her. "Are you going to call me Mummy? I like that."

Emma glowered at her. "Well, I *shan't*, because you're hateful and horrid."

"Fine," Briony said affably. "I'm hateful and horrid, and you're still going to bed."

"Daddy—" Emma turned to her father as to a court of final appeal, but he threw up his hands.

"She's the boss now," he said, indicating Briony.

Briony said quickly, "Suppose Daddy carries you up? You always like that."

Emma scowled harder, but let him pick her up. Briony followed them upstairs, while Emma glared at her over her father's shoulder. But when she was in bed she opened her arms to her and whispered, "I'm sorry, Mummy."

"That's all right," Briony said, laughing. "Now you've called me hateful and horrid I really feel like your mother."

"Can I truly call you Mummy? It's not too soon?"

"No, darling. It's not too soon." She looked at Carlyle. "I'll come down when Emma's asleep."

"Don't you want to go back to the party?" Emma asked.

"I'd much rather stay with you," Briony assured her.

Carlyle watched them a moment before leaving the room. Briony stayed until Emma had nodded off, then went downstairs to rejoin the family party.

"Is she all right?" Carlyle asked her in a low voice.

"Fine. We're the best of friends again, and she's sound asleep."

He smiled faintly and took both her hands in his. "I'm so glad I found you for Emma. I can't tell you—"

"You don't need to," she said quickly. "As long as Emma's happy, that's all that matters, isn't it?"

"Yes," he said fervently. "That's all that matters."

* * *

Next morning Emma was bright as a lark. Wearing her dressing gown she ran in just as Briony, assisted by Joyce, was putting on the bridal gown. Emma helped to do up the tiny buttons at the back, then watched in ecstasy as Joyce applied Briony's makeup.

"Now these," she said, indicating the string of flawless pearls that had been Carlyle's wedding gift. Briony had gasped when she saw them. Her own gift to him had been cuff links. They were platinum and had cleaned out her savings, but they paled beside the magnificence of the pearls.

"You put them on for me," Briony said. Frowning with concentration, Emma clasped them round her neck. "Did you help Daddy chose these?" Briony asked.

"Yes. He said they had to be the absolute best the shop had," Emma told her.

There was a knock on the door and Carlyle's voice called, "Briony—"

Emma shrieked and ran to the door. "No, Daddy, you mustn't come in." She darted out and they could hear her saying, "You mustn't see Mummy before you get to church."

And Carlyle saying prosaically, "But I see her every day."

"Not today," Emma lectured him. "It's unlucky. You want to be happy for years and years, don't you?"

"Yes, darling, of course." Briony could hear the awkwardness in his voice.

"She's happier than I've ever seen her," Joyce said. "And it's entirely due to you."

"She loves the excitement of a wedding. All little girls do."

"No, it's more than that. She loves you. Thank you for what you're doing, Briony." Joyce's face became wise. "My son has told me a little, but I'm sure he hasn't told me everything. Is this marriage a sacrifice for you?"

"No," Briony said quickly. "It's not a sacrifice. I love—I love Emma."

There was a pause before Joyce said quietly, "That's what I thought."

There was understanding in the older woman's eyes, and for a moment Briony almost dared to confide in her. But she was forestalled by a loud ring on the front doorbell.

"That will be the flowers," Joyce said. "I'll go and get them. I'm so glad we had this little talk."

"So am I," Briony said.

Joyce soon returned with the flowers. Briony had a bouquet of white roses. Instead of a posy Emma would carry a little basket of rose petals, and walk in front of the bride, strewing petals into her path.

When Emma was dressed she looked enchanting in her pink satin, with the material gathered into scalloped festoons around the hem. Pink rosebuds were gathered at her waist, and more buds adorned her hair. Something caught at Briony's heart at the thought that in a few months this enchanting little creature would exist no more. She pushed the thought firmly aside. Nothing must spoil this day for Emma.

At last Briony looked into the long mirror, and didn't recognize herself. The veil and gown framed her in a white mist, softening her angles, turning her into a fairy-tale creature. If she'd been dressing for a groom who loved her she would have rejoiced at the beautiful woman who looked back at her. But the marriage was a sham, and suddenly Briony felt its emptiness with a new pang.

There was another knock on the door and Carlyle called, "I'm about to leave for the church. Are you all ready?"

"Stop fussing, dear," his mother advised him, opening the door a crack. "You're not in your office now. I have everything under control. Off with you to the church."

He laughed and Briony heard his footsteps going downstairs. Looking out of the window, she saw him get into the long, black limousine, which glided away through the gates.

"I'll be going now, and leave you in Emma's capable hands," Joyce said. "Follow in five minutes."

Briony and Emma watched the bustling below. Joyce got into a car, with her husband and various cousins. More family members followed. At last only the bridal car awaited. Carlyle's uncle Derek, who was to give her away, knocked at the door. Briony said, "Ready?" Emma nodded and solemnly presented her with the bouquet.

It was a glorious day. The first leaves of autumn were beginning to fall, but they'd been blessed with an Indian summer, warm and sweet, and perfect for a wedding. On the short journey to church Briony tried to rid herself of a sense of unreality. But then, this *wasn't* real, just a parade of shadows. Somehow she must get through these next few months without allowing herself to fall in love with Carlyle. It would be the hardest thing she'd ever done in her life, for he was a man she could have loved, a man whose love she would have fought to win, if things had been different. But now she had no right to think of herself.

They'd reached the church. Emma hopped out of the car first and eased the train out, settling everything straight around Briony. Her little face was very serious

as she performed her duties. Then Briony took Uncle
Derek's arm and nodded for Emma to precede them into
the church.

As soon as they appeared in the doorway the organist
struck up "Here Comes the Bride." Walking into the
dim light straight from the sun Briony was momentarily
blinded. As her gaze cleared she could see Carlyle
standing at the altar. Emma was perfectly composed,
moving with grace and dignity as she sprinkled rose petals
from side to side. Carlyle stood motionless, a poignant
look on his face, as he witnessed the little procession
approach. It seemed as if something had taken his breath
away, and, recalling Emma's likeness to her mother,
Briony wondered if he was seeing Helen approach him.
She was glad he'd been given this beautiful moment to
remember from his daughter's short life.

At last Emma reached her father, stopped, then side-
stepped with great precision, making a space for the
bride. As Briony glided into position next to Carlyle he
looked directly at her and a faint smile softened his harsh
features. Something happened to her heart. She felt as
if the whole world had vanished, and she could do
nothing except stand here, looking into his eyes. She was
brought back to reality by a slight tug on her sleeve, and
looked down to find Emma waiting for the bouquet.
She handed it to her, and Emma stepped back, full of
grave responsibility.

Briony had steeled herself against the reciting of the
vows, but she had no defense against the moment when
Carlyle took her hand in his and held it there as he began
to say, "I, Carlyle David, take thee, Briony Anne, to be
my wedded wife, to have and to hold from this day
forward, for better, for worse..."

His voice faded. A tremor went through him. Briony felt it through the hand that gripped hers with sudden, terrible pressure, and she knew that a vision of the worst had come upon him, darkening the day, and making him cling to her instinctively.

In that moment the last of her detachment fell away. She couldn't stand aloof from this man, living with him day after day, witnessing his sorrow, and sharing it. She must love him with her whole heart and soul, giving endlessly with no hope of receiving. For only in that way could she help him. She felt courage flood through her. She was no green girl, but a woman, with a woman's power to love, and give, and endure. And she would put it all at the service of the man she loved.

Carlyle recovered himself and finished the vow. In a calm voice Briony made her promise, to have and to hold, for better, for worse, to love and to cherish. Her heart meant every word.

At last the vicar said, "You may kiss the bride," and Carlyle drew her close to lay his lips on hers. Briony tried to steady herself against the tide of love that swept through her. His mouth was warm and firm, touching hers gently for a kiss that might have lasted for a moment or for a hundred years. She couldn't be sure. She only knew that she loved him completely, and she always would.

As the organ pealed out a song of triumph, they turned and began the return march up the aisle, smiling for all the world to see. The photographer was waiting to catch the moment when they left the church, and there followed a seemingly endless series of pictures. Briony and Carlyle alone together, then with Emma standing in front, beaming.

"I'd like one alone with my daughter," Briony said, which made Emma ecstatic.

They found the perfect spot in the churchyard, beneath the trees. The photographer, who had a gift for spontaneity, snapped them walking hand-in-hand through a little flurry of leaves that a sudden wind had brought down, laughing together.

Then there were more poses with Carlyle's family, during one of which he murmured, "I took your advice."

"About what?" she whispered back.

"About taking *Emma's* advice. Wait until you see the surprise we have planned for you."

The surprise turned out to be an open, horse-drawn carriage. Briony laughed with delight, and Emma jumped for joy at her pleasure. Carlyle handed her in, but as he was about to close the door Briony said significantly, "You've forgotten something."

He understood at once and held out his hand to his daughter. "Get in."

"But the bride and groom are supposed to be alone," Emma said, torn between hope and tradition.

"You don't think we're going to shut you out from your own idea, do you?" he asked. "Come on."

Eagerly Emma seized his hand and jumped into the carriage. She sat facing them as they made the journey home, looking adoringly at Briony, and sometimes waving to people they passed in the streets, like visiting royalty. Little crowds gathered to watch them and wave back, enchanted by the picture the three of them presented.

"My daughter was right to make you buy that dress," Carlyle said, smiling.

"*Our* daughter," she said firmly.

"Yes. Our daughter has perfect taste."

"Mummy didn't want to buy it because she said it was far too expensive," Emma confided. "But I said it didn't matter *how* much it cost." She regarded her father with a touch of anxiety. "If it's too much, you can take it out of my pocket money."

He grinned. "Thank you, darling. I appreciate the offer, but I won't take it up. I don't care *how* much it cost. It's lovely. And so is Mummy."

"Yes, she is, isn't she?" said Emma happily.

At the reception speeches were made, toasts were drunk. Emma was allowed a sip of champagne, and toasted her new mother, her eyes shining with joy. The sight of that joy made everything worth it.

A cousin called Denis, whom Carlyle confided in an undervoice was the family clown, made a very funny speech which set the tables roaring with laughter. When the four strong band struck up, Denis made a low bow to Emma and led her onto the floor.

"She'll be all right with him," Carlyle said. "Denis is an idiot but a well-meaning idiot. Now, can I have a dance with my bride?"

As they were circling the floor Carlyle murmured, "You look wonderful. Everyone said so."

Did *you* think so? she wanted to ask. But at least she was here in his arms, held close in the bridal waltz.

"Your pearls were the finishing touch," she said. "I hadn't expected anything like this."

"Of course I gave you the best I could find. I wanted you to know that I— *Yes, it's been a great day, hasn't it?*" The last words were to someone who'd claimed his attention in passing. Briony sighed. What had he been going to say?

"How late are they going to stay?" he asked in her ear.

"I don't suppose they'll stay long, but we can hardly ask them to leave."

"Well, I wish they'd all go."

Her pulses began to race at the thought of what he might mean. When the music finished they each turned to other partners. Briony danced every dance in a dream. The room was hot and her heart was singing at the vision that had opened before her.

The evening drifted on. Carlyle danced with Emma, who was then sent, protesting, to bed. Denis claimed a waltz with Briony. He seemed to be in his late twenties, with mobile features and a great deal of volatile charm. He'd drunk too much champagne, which he frankly admitted. "That's the best thing about parties," he said cheerfully. "Chance to stock up at someone else's expense. Dashed if I ever thought to see Carlyle struck by love at first sight, though."

"Is that what he told you it was?" Briony asked casually.

"Carlyle? Go on. You know him better than that. Never talks about what's going on inside him. I don't think he's said more than fifty words to me in his life, and then they're usually terribly tragic things like, 'Not another penny,' and 'When are you going to get a proper job?'"

Briony chuckled. However feckless and unreliable Denis might be, his droll manner made him impossible to dislike.

"Then how do you know it was love at first sight?" she asked lightly.

"Well, look at the dates. He seems to have proposed almost as soon as he met you. Mind you, I don't blame him. If I'd met a smasher like you first I'd have proposed the same day."

Briony laughed out loud, causing several heads to turn. Carlyle's words had left her feeling too exhilarated to take offence at this irresponsible young man, and it was charming to be called 'a smasher' for the first time in her life.

"I don't think you ought to talk to me like that at my wedding," she teased.

"What, not call you a smasher? I can't help it. Look at yourself in the mirror and see how beautiful you are. Carlyle's a lucky dog." He tried to draw her close.

"Let me go at once," she ordered him, and he immediately relaxed his hold. "And be careful what Carlyle hears you say, or he won't make you another 'loan.'"

"Don't worry. I've already got that safe," he said with a wink, and she laughed again. Her head was swimming with delight. Soon the evening would end. Soon she would be alone with Carlyle.

Joyce announced the last waltz, and Carlyle took Briony in his arms again. He was frowning slightly. "You seem to get on well with Denis. Just don't believe anything he said to you."

"Not even when he told me I was beautiful?" she asked with a smile.

His face softened. "If you want compliments, I'm happy to pay you all you like. You've done me proud today." He drew her nearer. Her senses swam.

"What were you going to say to me?" she murmured.

"What?" He seemed to come out of a dream.

"You were going to tell me something about why you bought these pearls."

"Later. When everyone's gone. You do like them, don't you?"

"They're perfect."

"I told the jeweler they had to be." Carlyle gave a reminiscent grin. "He ended up ransacking three other branches of the shop before he found something that satisfied Emma and me. I think he was glad to see the back of us."

Was it madness to try to read something into Carlyle's desire to give her a perfect gift? Briony knew of his routine efficiency, but a little corner of her heart that persisted in believing in miracles, longed for something more. She touched the pearls gently, reveling in their beauty, hoping against hope...

Gradually the guests drifted away. The ones who were staying the night went to their rooms. Briony looked in on the sleeping Emma before going quietly to the bedroom she would share with Carlyle.

She'd chosen her nightdress with great care. If she could have pleased herself she would have selected something low-cut and seductive; a bride tempting her groom to the pleasures of passion. It would have been sweet and wonderful to know that Carlyle would look on her with the eyes of love; to don a wispy garment that his eager hands would toss aside in the urgency of his desire; then to lie with him in the warmth of the big bed, giving and receiving pleasure until exhaustion overtook them and they could sleep in each other's arms.

But she hadn't dared to wear such a nightdress for fear of embarrassing him. Nor, on the other hand, did she want to seem dowdy. Their situation might indicate cotton or flannel buttoned to the neck, but she would have died rather. Finally she'd settled on peach satin trimmed with lace. The neck was modest by bridal standards, but a tug on a dainty ribbon would open it further. What he read into it would depend on how he felt.

And after his words earlier, she could hope. She touched the pearls that were still around her neck, glowing against her pale skin. He'd said, *I wanted you to know that I—* What was it he wanted her to know?

At last she heard his footsteps coming along the hall from the bathroom, where he'd changed. Her heart was beating with thrilling anticipation as he opened the door. He was wearing a wine-colored silk dressing gown over dark blue pajamas. He smiled when he saw her sitting at the dressing table, and came over to look into the mirror over her head.

"What a day!" he said. "I shall be glad when the last of them have gone tomorrow and we can have the house to ourselves."

"So shall I," she said fervently.

"No regrets? It's not going to be too much for you, is it?"

She met his eyes in the mirror. "I have no regrets, Carlyle, and I never will have."

"Nor me." He smiled and touched the pearls. Briony's heart was beating so hard she was sure he could hear it. At any moment now he would say something that would fill her with delight. "Take care of these, won't you?"

"I will," she told him softly.

"Let me help you with them."

She felt him working on the clasp, his fingers brushing against the nape of her neck, and wild thrills went through her. She looked anxiously at her reflection, sure that the warmth that had surged up in her could be seen on her skin. But the woman in the mirror looked back calmly. Only her shining eyes betrayed that she was alight with love, longing to believe that her dreams could come true.

"There," Carlyle said at last. "It might be an idea to put them in a bank for safety."

"But I'd rather keep them with me. They're so lovely."

"They're also very valuable. In time you should be able to sell them for quite a lot."

At the word "sell" the dream shattered, revealing itself as tinsel after all. Briony watched, stunned, as the pieces drifted to the ground, to be trodden underfoot.

"Sell them?" she managed to ask. "Why would I want to do that?"

"Why not? My dear, it's all right. I don't expect you to be sentimental about my gifts. We made a bargain, and you're keeping your side wonderfully. I couldn't have asked for more." As she turned to stare at him he touched her face, gently lifting her chin. "You're a generous woman, Briony, with a great heart. One day, some man's going to be very lucky."

She smiled faintly. "Was that what you were going to say to me?"

"Partly, but there's something else. Here." He reached into a drawer and pulled out an envelope.

"It looks like my bank statement," she said, puzzled.

"It is. It came this morning but I kept it to give to you myself. You might get a surprise."

Pulling it open, Briony stared at the amount there. "But—"

"It's more than the monthly salary we agreed I should pay you—"

"It's nearly double."

"I decided to show my gratitude in tangible form."

Briony felt as if she'd received a blow in the stomach. It was for this that her pulses had raced as she climbed the stairs to their bedroom. "There was no need—" she began to say.

But Carlyle forestalled her, putting the bank statement aside and taking both her hands in his. "You don't understand," he said fervently. "When I see how you've transformed Emma's life, how much you've done for her—I just feel that nothing is too good for you." He waited for her to react, puzzled by her pallor and stillness. "Did I make a mistake?" he asked, attempting a joke. "Isn't it enough?"

She wanted to scream, "No, it's not enough. I want much more. I want your heart. I want you to look at me with the tenderness you give Emma. I want your love and your need. I want all of you. And you fob me off with money."

But she only smiled and said, "Don't be silly. It's far too much."

"I don't think it's too much for the woman who's making my Emma happy." He dropped a light kiss on the top of her head. "I'm glad everything's all right again. For a moment I thought I'd done something wrong. Now, let's get to bed. I shall sleep like a log tonight. Which side do you prefer?"

Silently, fighting to hide her cruel disappointment, Briony got into bed. Carlyle got into the other side and put out the light. For a while they both lay without speaking or moving, until at last she could tell by his breathing that he'd fallen asleep. Only then could she relax. Her body was aching from the effort of holding it still. Just a foot away from her lay Carlyle, her love and yet not her love. That twelve inches was like a chasm, but he was still close enough for her to be intensely aware of him. Suddenly she wondered how she was going to endure this marriage.

CHAPTER SIX

BRIONY had made an instant hit with Nora and Tom, who together took care of the house and garden, leaving her free to concentrate on Emma. Often in the afternoons she would have a snack with them in the kitchen. It was a large room, with a superficially traditional air that came from the copper pans that hung around the walls. But despite this the gadgetry was state-of-the-art.

"It's like the deck of a space station," Briony said once, looking around at all the knobs and lights. "Did Carlyle put this in for you?" For she knew that Nora lived for her cooking.

"Some of the most recent stuff was put in because I asked for it," Nora said. "But it was always the latest gadgetry. Helen—" She stopped delicately.

"Helen wanted it that way," Briony finished for her. "It's all right. You needn't be afraid to mention her to me. Did you know her well?"

"We met at the same cordon bleu cookery class," Nora said. "Later she asked Tom and me to come and work for her. They'd just got married and were doing up this house."

"She looks lovely in her pictures," Briony observed casually. She was alone with Nora today, and felt able to talk more freely than with Tom around.

"Oh, she was beautiful," Nora remembered. "So dainty and delicate, as if a breath would blow her away. When she died, I thought he'd go crazy. I'm sure he *would* have gone crazy but for the little one."

When the enlargements of the photographs arrived Briony and Nora went through them together. Nora was entranced by the one of Emma and Briony.

"She looks such a little angel," she sighed. "You'd never guess—" She broke off with a wry smile.

"No, but I'm finding out," Briony said.

Despite the weakening effect of her illness, Emma was no angel but a normal child. She was sweet-natured, and there wasn't an unkind bone in her body, but she was also stubborn to the point of mulishness. She had a strong will and the ability to focus her attention like a laser onto the serious business of getting her own way. In short, she was Carlyle in miniature.

Her father found it hard to say no to her, and impossible to rebuke her. Briony knew that she had to tread a very fine line. Emma could indulge in a battle of wills so exhausting that it became dangerous for her. The little monkey wasn't above using her frailty as a weapon, with the result that she prevailed too often and was getting out of hand.

Yet, even when she was at her most infuriating, Emma was never less than lovable. Sometimes Briony would catch her glancing secretly at her in the midst of an argument, as though this were no more than a game that the two of them were playing. When this happened they would often burst into laughter together, and the conviction grew on Briony that she was being tested.

"You're a little wretch," she said once.

"A terrible wretch?" Emma asked hopefully.

"The worst little wretch in the whole world."

"In the whole uni-uni—?"

"Universe," Briony confirmed as Emma reached for her notepad. "In fact, the worst in the whole galaxy." She spelled both words and waited until Emma had written them before adding, "But if you were ten times the wretch you are I'd still love you, so eat up your greens and stop trying to discover my limits, because you'll never find them."

And Emma's gleeful look told her she'd got it right.

Emma was intelligent and eager to learn, and she took her dictionary very seriously. The little notebook went everywhere with her, and she could stop an adult conversation dead in its tracks by demanding to have a word explained and spelled.

She attended school only in the mornings. At lunchtime Briony collected her, and Emma would spend the afternoon resting on her bed, reading until she fell asleep. By the time Carlyle returned in the evening she was refreshed and eager to chat to him over supper.

Sometimes they would take her to the ballet. Carlyle was bored by ballet but he sat through everything, ignoring the stage, his eyes fixed on Emma, savouring her wide-eyed delight.

One evening he brought home a Camcorder, which Emma pounced on with glee. The three of them sorted out the instructions, got it all wrong, laughed a lot, and finally cracked the secret. Emma filmed them to her heart's content and he let her hog the machine. But at last he said, "Let me take some of you," speaking casually so that she wouldn't guess he was storing up pictures for the time when pictures were all he would have.

Often Briony would see him laughing with Emma as though he hadn't a care in the world. Afterward, in the privacy of their room, his shoulders would sag and his face would be gray with strain. She longed to comfort him, but knew in her heart that it was useless. There was no comfort for the death of a beloved child.

On November the fifth Briony held a fireworks party for Emma's school friends. The evening was a huge success. Emma was in high spirits, bonneted, scarved and mittened, drawing patterns in the darkness with sparklers.

"Daddy, look at me," she cried, waving one so close to his face that he only just retreated in time.

"Don't poke my eye out," he laughed. "Here, let me have a go."

He struck matches and suddenly the air was alive with the glitter of multicolored sparklers, illuminating both their faces as if by magic. They were smiling at each other in a perfect moment that excluded the rest of the world. Briony caught it on camera and, later that night, when the house was asleep, she went downstairs to play the tape. There was Carlyle, his face alight with love and tenderness for his child. It was a look Briony had seen often, but never turned toward herself.

As the year drew to a close, the volume of work in Carlyle's office increased, and he began bringing it home. One evening Briony went into his study with coffee and sandwiches while he was on the phone. After setting the snack down she would have departed, but, without looking at her, he waved an imperious hand for her to wait.

Just as if I were still his secretary, she thought, between indignation and amusement.

She'd grown so used to the tender father and conscientious husband that she'd almost forgotten the other Carlyle, the autocrat who barked orders to underlings. She sat down while he finished tying up his arrangements. While she waited she noticed a paper on the edge of the desk, and the name George Cosway leapt out at her. She remembered it from that first day when Carlyle had called her into his office to alter the Cosway contract. Out of curiosity she glanced over the document.

"I don't care if you have to get him out of bed," Carlyle was saying into the phone. "I'm not waiting any longer. Get me an answer by tomorrow." He was briefly silent. "Don't argue, Sam. Do it." Another short silence. "Just *do* it," he snapped and hung up.

Briony chuckled. "We used to call you The Great Fixer in the office," she recalled. "The legend was that you could fix anything."

"So I should hope." He leaned back, his arms behind his head, grinning. He was on a "high" from having forced matters to go the way he wanted, for him the most potent drug in the world. "It's incredible how often life is just a matter of pulling a few strings behind the scenes—"

"Moving a few people about as pawns—" she teased him. His mood was infectious.

"That, too," he conceded. "I have a theory that life is divided into the pawns and the movers."

"With you as the mover and everyone else as the pawns," Briony said. "You got *me* doing what you wanted."

"Of course. That's how I like it. In a well-ordered world everyone would be doing what I wanted."

Then, abruptly, his exhilaration died. "But some things can't be fixed," he said somberly. "Not even for the toughest mover in town."

Briony met his eyes, and what she saw in them hurt her. Behind the knock'em-flat philosophy and the cheerful ruthlessness, Carlyle was slowly dying inside. And she, who'd longed to comfort his pain, was powerless against it. As powerless as he was himself.

At last he sighed and said, "It took me a long time to accept that there's something I can't do anything about, but I guess I'm getting there. Is she asleep?"

"She ought to be, but I think she'll stay awake hoping you'll look in for a good-night kiss."

"All right, I'll go up in a minute. Ah, coffee! Great." He poured himself a cup and glanced at the paper she was still holding. "What do you think of that?"

"I'm sorry," she said quickly. "I didn't mean to pry. I just happened to notice Cosway's name and wondered how that contract had come out."

"Not too well. He's still making difficulties. Don't apologize. I don't mind you looking. I haven't forgotten."

"Forgotten what?"

"Our bargain. I promised you business opportunities in return for your time in this marriage."

"You're already paying me a big salary."

"But I want to give you more than that. You have the makings of a first-rate assistant. For me, perhaps."

Out of sight Briony clenched her hands. How could he talk about working together later, as though nothing had happened? "I don't think that would be a very good idea," she said.

"No? Perhaps not. I just wanted you to know that I'm a man of my word. You were right to remind me."

"I didn't—I was just—"

"No, not deliberately. But you're still interested in business, aren't you? I'll give you some books to read. You'll find them helpful."

"Thank you," Briony said dully.

The sweet comradeship of a moment ago was gone. To make matters worse Carlyle immediately turned to the bookshelf behind him and pulled down a volume.

"Aspects Of Management," he said. "Start with this. Now I'll go up and say good-night to Emma."

A stranger walking into the Brackman household would have thought they saw the perfect family. The love that joined both parents to the child was an almost tangible thing, infusing the whole house with its atmosphere. Briony devoted herself to Emma's care, taking her to and from school, overseeing her rest, talking to her. Carlyle came home each day as early as he could, and if he brought work with him he never did it until his daughter was tucked up in bed.

Often he would have a snack in his study and work far into the night. Sometimes he would eat with his wife, and discuss their daughter. Usually she went to bed first while he made a few trans-Atlantic phone calls, and at last he would enter quietly and get into bed without putting the light on, so as not to wake her.

In fact, she was never asleep, although she pretended to be. Beneath the untroubled surface of their lives Briony was tense with sadness and longing. Her unsatisfied love tormented her. At first it had been almost enough to see Carlyle every day. There was joy in loving him and being constantly in his company, and that alone buoyed her up for a while. But gradually the need for more became overwhelming.

If she wanted to talk about Emma he would set aside everything else. His dark eyes would be fixed on Briony intently, and occasionally he would smile. For a brief moment she could pretend that it was she herself who entranced him. But reality was always waiting to destroy the illusion, and she would find herself left alone again, in a place that increasingly felt like a desert.

He liked her, he was grateful to her, and he showed that gratitude generously. And after that one explosion when he'd ended the engagement he was always courteous and considerate. But there was nothing else. She had to face that fact.

At first it had hardly mattered that she was living in Helen's house. But as the excitement of the wedding faded she became more aware that this was where Carlyle had brought his bride, ten years ago, the house they'd done up together. In an unguarded moment Nora had let slip that nothing was allowed to change. If the decorations grew shabby they were replaced exactly as they had been. There'd been some updating in the kitchen, but apart from that everything was as Helen had chosen it. And Briony wondered how much a man would have to love a woman to stop the clock on the day of her death.

Once, searching for a pen she'd lent him, she'd ventured to open the drawers of his desk in the study. And there she'd found something she would rather not have seen. It was a photograph of Helen, with her baby in her arms, taken, Briony knew, by Carlyle himself. She'd looked frail and near to death, but still beautiful. Briony had seen this picture beside Carlyle's bed, but he'd courteously removed it before their marriage. Now she knew that he'd hidden it here where he could brood over it privately.

Beneath the picture was a photo album. Briony wrestled with temptation, but in the end no power on earth could have stopped her jealously turning the pages. There was Carlyle and Helen on their wedding day, their faces radiant as they gazed at each other. There they were on holiday, Helen in a bikini, held high in his arms, shrieking with laughter as he prepared to toss her into the water.

It was hard to recognize Carlyle. The sharp-tongued autocrat he'd become had been little more than a boy in those days, with a candid, glowing face, untouched by grief. Briony felt as if she could see into his mind. He was young, talented, passionately in love, and he'd been granted his heart's desire. He believed the world was his, and it always would be. He had no idea how tragically soon his happiness was to be snatched from him. Sadly, Briony put the pictures away.

One night, as so often before, she lay still and wakeful long after Carlyle had gone to sleep. The bed, which had seemed large enough from the outside, was far too small now they were sharing it. It was impossible not to be conscious of his big body so close to hers, clad only in thin pajamas, sharing the same warmth as her own.

The moonlight gave her a clear view of his face, so tense in the daytime, so vulnerable in sleep. She had to fight the temptation to lay her lips gently on his and enjoy one forbidden kiss. As she watched the shape of his mouth, unexpectedly curved in contrast to his harsh features, she could feel it against her own as it had been during their wedding. Memory pervaded her, flooding her body with desire. In another moment she would lean forward and brush his lips with hers...

Briony clenched her hands and forced herself to leave the bed. She must get away from Carlyle until this dangerous mood had passed. Moving quietly, she took her dressing gown and slipped out. Downstairs she fetched *Aspects Of Management*, and went to the kitchen. There she made herself some hot milk and sat staring at the book until she realized she'd read the same page four times without taking anything in. Words danced before her. They were sharp, like little arrows to plunge into her heart. The world was full of torment and there was nothing she could do to ease it.

"What are you doing down here so late?"

She looked up quickly to see Carlyle standing in the doorway in his pajamas, his hair tousled, his chin beginning to look unshaven. Her heart did a dangerous somersault.

She pulled herself together. "Where are your slippers?" she demanded, pointing accusingly at his bare feet.

He grinned. "Don't talk to me as if I was Emma."

"Emma has more good sense than you. She puts her slippers on because she knows the weather's turning cold."

"She puts her slippers on because you bought her a pair done up to look like her favorite cartoon characters." He yawned and rubbed his eyes. "What are you drinking? Is there any left?"

"Sit down." She went to the hob while he pulled her book over and examined it.

"You're a conscientious student," he said. "Or do I mean ambitious?"

"It's a fascinating subject," she said, avoiding his question. "I do a lot of reading while Emma's at school. Do you want anything in your hot milk?"

"Cocoa, if we have any."

She laughed as she set the mug before him, and seated herself. "If your rivals could see you now. They all think you eat people for breakfast."

"That's what I want them to think."

"I know. Cocoa would ruin your image."

He grinned. "Well, let's keep it our secret."

It wasn't fair, she thought, that he should get out of bed, rumpled and disordered, and be twice as attractive as when he was elegantly dressed. Carlyle could be thrilling when he presented his imperious face to the world, but Briony loved him best as he was now, looking younger and more vulnerable. She was filled with a sudden passion of tenderness, and it was an effort not to put her arms around him.

He sipped, and said appreciatively, "You make cocoa as you do everything else, with total efficiency. What's your secret?"

"Emma taught me how you like it. By the way, has she told you about her latest idea? She wants to join the Brownies."

He set his mug down sharply. "No way. Have you seen what those kids get up to? Climbing trees and running about—"

"Will you calm down?"

"Not until this damn fool idea is hit on the head, once and for all."

"We'll let the doctor tell us if it's a damn fool idea."

"*I'm* telling you—"

"Well, don't," Briony said firmly. "We had this out once before. You may be Emma's father but I'm her mother. Now hush, and listen to me. Emma's lonely. She leaves school at midday, so she doesn't get to socialize with the others at lunchtime, or join in their activities. I know that can't be helped, but she needs the company of other children."

"It's too risky."

"It needn't be. I'll talk to the Brownie leader and explain that there are things she can't do. And I'll be there to keep an eye on her, and take her away if I think she's getting tired. Trust me." She gave him an impish smile. "You should know better than to try to bully me."

Carlyle's face was a picture of outraged innocence. "Bully? *Me?* I'm the mildest of men."

"Ha! You hit the roof if you don't get your own way." Briony was openly laughing at him. "And you try to ride over me in hobnailed boots. I can see just where Emma gets it from."

He grinned ruefully. "She *is* like me, isn't she?"

"Exactly."

For once the moment wasn't overshadowed by grief for the future. They exchanged a smile, full of their shared love for the little girl. Carlyle reached out his hand and she took it. Then his smile died, and a surprised look came into his eyes. He stayed like that, studying her, frowning a little, as if trying to come to terms with a new idea. Then his hand tightened, and the next moment he leaned forward and kissed her.

It happened so quickly that Briony had no chance to steel herself not to react. Instinctively her lips softened and parted against his, while longing flooded her whole body. There was sweetness in the way he'd reached out to her now, not as a show for Emma's benefit, but in the warmth of companionship and need. He slipped his free hand behind her head, running his fingers through her hair and drawing her closer to him so that the pressure of his mouth intensified. Briony knew that she should stop this now. It meant little to him except that he was lonely and sad, and she was there. He thought her feelings were as moderate as his own, never guessing the volcano of love that lived within her, threatening to erupt at any moment. He was taking her closer to that moment, and she must fight it for both their sakes—for Emma's sake. But not yet—not yet—

He rose to his feet, drawing her with him. The kiss changed, became deeper and more intense. "Briony..." he murmured her name.

"Yes," she whispered.

His lips were insistently persuasive, teasing her to open her mouth for him. All her stern resolution seemed to slip away from her and she let her lips fall helplessly apart. She could feel the hard leanness of his body through the thin material of their nightclothes. Excitement flooded her as she thought how this could end. She was more than Emma's mother. She was a woman, passionately in love with a man, prepared to do anything to win his love.

As his tongue slowly caressed the inside of her mouth, her desire almost overwhelmed her. She pressed against him, feeling the heat of his flesh communicate itself to hers. His spicy, masculine smell excited her, making the blood pound in her veins, and her limbs turn to water.

His lips burned a trail of fire down her neck to her throat. Her chest was rising and falling as her breathing became slow and languorous. The skin of her whole body seemed to have come alive. In another minute he would drop his head further, tear away the material to kiss her breasts. And she wanted that so much. She wanted everything. She wanted him. All of him. Heart, mind, soul and body. Would it really be wrong to use their enforced closeness to seek a way to his heart? Didn't she have the right to try? At this moment he wanted her, too. It would be so easy to melt into his arms, to climb the broad stairs to their room, to their bed...

And afterward? When she'd revealed her love to a man who couldn't love her in return, and passion was replaced by the cold light of dawn? What then? They could never be natural and unembarrassed with each other afterward, and the one to suffer would be Emma.

"Briony," Carlyle murmured again, and suddenly his arms tightened, drawing her against him in a crushing embrace, while his mouth teased and tormented hers with promises of delight.

For a blazingly sweet instant she hovered on the brink of yielding. But then common sense came to her rescue and she stiffened against him, pushing against his chest with her hands. "No," she said in a muffled voice. "Carlyle—please—don't do this."

He stopped, not releasing her, but as though too surprised to know what to do. "Let me go," she whispered.

He looked into her face. "You don't mean that—"

"I do." She fought for control but it was hard when he was still holding her close. "Please let me go. You promised."

He expelled his breath, and his hands fell away from her. "Yes, I did, of course." His voice had an odd, flat quality. "I thought I'd read you right, but obviously I made a mistake." He took a step away from her. "I apologize."

"There's no need for that—" she said haltingly.

"Of course there is. We made a bargain and bargains are sacred. I live my life on that principle. I can't think how I came to— Try to forgive my bad manners."

She could have wept. This was all so wrong, so far from what she wanted. But the next moment things grew worse. Carlyle glanced at the book Briony had been trying to read when he found her, and his mouth twisted in a wry smile of understanding. She wanted to cry out that it wasn't the way he thought, but there was nothing she could say.

"Don't get upset," he told her in a rallying tone. "I just got carried away and forgot the rules. It won't happen again. I give you my word."

CHAPTER SEVEN

THE doctor cleared Emma for joining the Brownies, as long as Briony was there to ensure that she didn't do too much. Faced with Emma's delight, Carlyle reluctantly backed down. Thereafter, each Wednesday evening Emma attended Brownies for an hour and came home in the seventh heaven. She learned a series of knots, which she explained to Carlyle until he declared he could do them in his sleep, and she went round the house singing campfire songs until the adults put cotton wool in their ears. Everyone was happy.

Joyce telephoned several times a week, and Briony enjoyed these calls. She'd quickly developed a real affection for her outspoken mother-in-law.

Near the end of November, Carlyle threw a small party for Briony to meet his friends. "I should call them acquaintances, myself," Joyce said when Briony told her. "He seldom gets close enough to people to make real friendships."

"That's how it seems to me," Briony agreed. "I wondered if he'd just drawn back into himself since Emma grew so ill."

"He has, but he was always a bit that way. I wish you the best of luck in the lion's den. Watch out for Deirdre Raye. She's recently divorced, and she'd convinced herself that Carlyle was only waiting for her to be free to pop the question. Nonsense, of course. He'd have asked her long ago if he'd wanted her. She's been in the

States, and probably didn't even hear about the wedding until she came back. She'll be as angry as a snake."

Being direct by nature, Briony told Carlyle about this conversation as they went to bed that night, making a joke of it. He looked surprised.

"I should think my tactless mother has got the wrong end of the stick. Deirdre's divorce had nothing to do with me, and I'm sure she's never thought of me in that way."

"You weren't going to 'pop the question' then?"

"Certainly not. For one thing, Emma doesn't like her. I can't think why, because Deirdre's always gone out of her way to be nice to her, but when Emma takes one of her unreasonable dislikes you can't budge her."

"So Deirdre's out on Emma's say-so," Briony mused.

"Deirdre was never in," Carlyle said, looking faintly annoyed.

"According to Joyce, she thinks she was. Sure you didn't give her cause?"

"I've flirted with her at parties, but only in the way we all do. It's a kind of meaningless routine."

"Well, if you don't want your drink spiked with arsenic, don't flirt with her at this party," Briony advised him darkly.

"I wasn't going to," he said. "Emma would hate it."

The day before the party Nora buried herself in the kitchen and began a whirlwind of culinary preparation. Although she was the hostess Briony knew better than to interfere with genius, and confined herself to assisting. The result was a buffet of real splendor.

The wines were chosen. The crystal glasses were set out. Emma's "party best" was her bridesmaid dress. Briony wore her wedding pearls and, at Carlyle's urging, had splashed out on an elegant blue silk cocktail dress. It was wickedly extravagant but worth every penny for the way it enhanced her. She knew she could bear comparison with Carlyle's friends, but she was still nervous.

There were about fifty guests. Some were business colleagues, others were local people. They were all expensively dressed and sleekly well-fed. Every woman sized Briony up, mentally appraised the dress and costed the pearls. At first her hackles were inclined to rise, but gradually it became clear that they approved of her. The atmosphere grew friendlier, especially when Sylvia, a distant cousin of Carlyle's who'd been at the wedding, arrived and greeted her with enthusiasm. Sylvia was a jolly, boisterous young woman with no tact, but a warm heart, and her endorsement smoothed Briony's path.

But under the pleasant hum there was an air of expectancy. Everyone was waiting for one particular guest, eager to see the meeting between the two women.

Deirdre arrived late. Carlyle had vanished into the study to show off his new computer to anyone interested. So Briony met Deirdre alone, and knew at once that Joyce's advice had been good. The other woman's eyes narrowed in surprise and displeasure, as though she'd been expecting a little brown mouse and found the well-groomed reality a shock.

Deirdre's own appearance was all that money could buy. She was a tall woman in her early thirties, with blue-black hair and features that might have been beautiful if they hadn't been so hard. On her wrist and in her ears she wore rubies set in gold that were obviously real and worth a fortune. Briony put her head up and greeted her with composure.

"I was fascinated to hear that Carlyle had married on the spur of the moment," Deirdre cooed. "It's so unlike him. Those of us who know him best know that he hasn't a romantic bone in his body.''

Briony had a split second to decide how to handle the silky malice that gleamed from Deirdre's eyes. There and then she decided that if this woman wanted battle, she could have it.

''Well, maybe those who know him best don't know him as well as they think they do,'' she said sweetly, and was rewarded by a muffled giggle from Sylvia. Deirdre's mouth stretched a little further, but her eyes were cold.

''Let me get you a drink,'' Briony said, taking her by the arm. She guided her out of the crowd and furnished her with a glass. The two women surveyed each other.

''Now don't be cross with me if I put my foot in it,'' Deirdre said sweetly. ''I think your wedding is a perfectly lovely story, and I'm so glad to meet you at last. It's just that I've known dear Carlyle for so long, and been so close to him that—well, you won't mind if I give you the teensiest little bit of advice, will you?''

''I might,'' Briony said, so affably that at first Deirdre didn't take her meaning. She gave a chilly laugh and said, ''Oh, nobody takes offence at the things I say.''

''You amaze me,'' Briony said, still in the same pleasant tone. ''What is your teensy little bit of advice?''

Deirdre leaned forward until her expensively coiffed hair was almost touching Briony's. ''Don't try to separate him from his friends,'' she said conspiratorially. ''You're bound to feel a bit left out at first, but a man like Carlyle will never tolerate being dictated to.''

''But I don't feel left out,'' Briony told her. ''Carlyle's friends have made me very welcome.''

''His real friends, that is,'' Sylvia put in sweetly.

Deirdre gave a small, tense smile, but before she could respond Emma had appeared. Deirdre gave an affected cry of delight. "*There's* my darling little girl. Don't you look enchanting? Come here, dearie, I simply must hug you."

Emma backed off, but she wasn't quick enough. Deirdre swooped down like a bird of prey and smothered her with kisses. "Oh, you poor, sweet thing. You're still so frail."

"I'm *not*," Emma said, rubbing her mouth on the back of her hand. "I'm ever so much better."

Deirdre sighed. "So brave."

"You heard Emma," Briony said firmly. "She's better. We can all see it."

"Of course, of course," Deirdre concurred, but in a too hasty, theatrical manner that would have told a much less intelligent child than Emma that she meant just the opposite.

"Darling, will you tell Daddy Mrs. Raye is here?" Briony asked her.

When she'd scampered off, Deirdre said, "Actually 'Raye' was my husband's name, but I don't use it now I'm free. I've gone back to my maiden name, Grant."

"Very well, Miss Grant," Briony said. Beneath her composed exterior she was furiously angry. How dare this woman risk confronting Emma with the truth simply to score a cheap point! "I'd prefer it if you didn't talk about Emma looking frail. Those aren't the kind of thoughts Carlyle and I wish her to dwell on."

"Carlyle and I," Deirdre mused, her head slightly on one side. "You say that so naturally. Once—ah, well, never mind."

"I won't," Briony said. She was discovering that these blunt rejoinders served her well. Deirdre was clearly more at home with deviousness and found plain speaking hard to cope with. "But please understand that I mean it," she continued. "Emma comes first."

"But of course she does," Deirdre declared, wide-eyed. "We all understand that. After all, that's why—I mean, we don't talk about it, but— *Carlyle*, my dearest." She advanced on Carlyle who was coming through the crowd, her hands outstretched. She enfolded him in a scented hug which he returned, smiling. "Oh, I've been dying to see if marriage has changed you."

"Ask my wife," he said, indicating Briony with a smile.

"It hasn't," Briony informed the assembled company. "He's still overbearing and tyrannical."

"Overbearing," Emma repeated ecstatically. "And tyr-tyr—"

"Tyrannical, darling," Briony said. "I'll give you the spelling later."

"Thanks, the pair of you," Carlyle said, to laughter.

Deirdre tucked her hand into Carlyle's arm and drew him away. "We must have a nice long talk. I'm just dying to hear—"

They vanished, arm in arm.

The party swirled and eddied, bringing Briony together with Carlyle, then pulling them apart. Once, as their paths crossed for a moment, she murmured to him, "You were right. Emma can't stand her, and with good reason. Fancy calling her 'dearie', and saying she was 'a poor, sweet thing.'"

Carlyle grinned. "Did she say that?"

"She did. You should have seen Emma's face!"

"I wish I had."

They laughed together. Deirdre, watching them, grew very still.

Some of the guests were going through the wedding albums. Deirdre drifted across as though barely interested, but her gaze, as she examined the pictures, reminded Briony of a hawk.

"Oh, look at Emma," Deirdre sighed. "Isn't she a little angel?"

Briony felt Emma grow tense and hastened to say, "You don't want to be fooled by that innocent face. She's not a little angel, she's a little terror." Emma relaxed, evidently finding this far more acceptable.

Nora entered with more food and the crowd swirled toward her, leaving Briony and Deirdre alone with the album.

"Such lovely pearls," Deirdre sighed. "I can see why you can't bear to take them off."

"They were Carlyle's wedding gift," Briony said politely.

Deirdre smiled. "He has perfect taste. He knows exactly what jewels to chose for a woman, doesn't he?" She raised the wrist bearing the ruby bracelet and touched one of her earrings. The message was unmistakable. Deirdre was saying that these, too, had been Carlyle's gifts. Briony felt sick, but she managed to smile.

It didn't matter if Carlyle had given this overblown woman jewels, she told herself. It was in the past, and anyway, she had no right to mind. But what hurt was that he'd deceived her about it.

Unless Deirdre was lying. But the next moment Deirdre sashayed across the room to Carlyle and held up the rubies, purring, "You see, I still have your lovely gift..."

"So I should hope," he said.

Briony thought of herself as a calm, controlled person, but there was nothing controlled about the passion of jealousy that overwhelmed her now. She hated that woman, not only because she wore Carlyle's jewels, but because Deirdre was part of his life that she herself knew nothing about.

I've got to stop this, she thought wildly. I'm steady, efficient Briony, doing a job. Nothing else.

But "old reliable" had vanished, drowned in a torrent of misery.

"Mummy," said Emma plaintively at her side, "I don't like Auntie Deirdre. I never did."

Briony pulled herself together. "Neither do I, darling. And I'll give you some more words for your dictionary. Scheming, spiteful, two-faced and devious."

"She's also a rattlesnake," Sylvia observed.

Emma beamed. "Rattle—"

"You forget that one," Briony commanded her quickly. "Sylvia, don't encourage her. In any case, it's bedtime."

"Oh, please, Mummy, just a few more minutes."

"Five."

"Fifteen."

"Ten."

"Done."

They shook hands on it, just as Carlyle appeared, saying, "Isn't it time she was in bed?"

"We've just done a deal," Briony told him. "Ten minutes."

He gave a wry grin. "And when ten minutes is up, what will the excuse be then?"

"I'll think of something," Emma promised, smiling seraphically from one to the other.

"She will, too," Carlyle prophesied, tweaking his daughter's hair affectionately.

"I'm sure she won't," Deirdre declared, just behind Carlyle. "You'll be a good little girl and go right off to bed, won't you, dear?"

"No, I won't," Emma said, setting her chin in a way that meant trouble. "Mummy says I'm a terror. And I am."

"Don't be silly," Deirdre cooed. "Of course you're not."

"Yes, I *am*."

Deirdre gave Briony a look of sad wisdom. "Is it wise to call the child names? If she knows the worst is expected of her she—"

"Mummy's good at calling people names," Emma explained cheerfully. "She called Daddy overbearing and tyrannical, and she said you were dev—"

"Emma," Briony said quickly.

"Well, she is," Emma said mutinously, before falling silent.

Even then the moment might have passed, but for the chuckles in the assembled guests, few of whom liked Deirdre. They were hastily muffled, but not fast enough to prevent their object hearing them, and understanding their meaning. Deirdre looked around her, and made the mistake of losing her temper.

"If you ask me," she said frigidly to Carlyle, "your daughter is getting entirely out of hand. Because she's ill you let her do and say whatever she likes, and it's a big mistake."

"I apologize if you're offended," Briony said coolly. "Nobody intended that to happen."

"She did," Deirdre snapped, pointing at Emma, who stood, a small, martyred saint, regarding the proceedings. "The little beast has always tried to get under my skin." She rounded on Briony. "I'm not taken in by

her 'cute' little ways, even if you are. She shouldn't be out amongst decent people. There are places that cope with children like her—"

Carlyle's brow darkened with anger, but before he could speak Briony forestalled him. "How dare you speak about Emma like that!" she snapped. "She's a perfectly normal child who happens to be a little unwell—"

Deirdre sniffed. "Normal. That's not what I'd call it."

"You can call it whatever you like, as long as you don't do so here," Briony said coolly. "Good night, Miss Grant. The door is behind you."

Deirdre gasped. "You can't do that. I'm a guest. Carlyle invited me—"

"And I'm throwing you out," Briony declared. "Nobody who speaks of my daughter like that is a guest as long as I'm mistress of this house. *Good night*."

Deirdre looked at Carlyle for help, but he stayed silent, regarding her from cold eyes. Head up, she turned and went to the front door before delivering her final shot. "But just how long do you think you'll be mistress of this house?" Then she swept out, banging the front door behind her.

Briony prepared for bed that night in a rage. The tensions of the evening had finally boiled over when she was alone. She stripped off the beautiful dress and put on her satin nightgown, the one she'd worn on her wedding night. With a slight feeling of bitterness she checked that the bow at the neck was safely fastened.

When she'd hung up her things she almost slammed the wardrobe door. Carlyle, entering in time to see this, found himself confronted with a Briony he'd never met before. Her eyes were stormy and there was a sharp precision in her movements that denoted a woman in a furious temper. He hung up his dressing gown, waiting for her to speak. When she didn't, he tested the ground cautiously.

"It was a great party," he said.

"Good."

"You were a real success. I was proud of you."

"Good."

"You're very monosyllabic. Is something wrong?"

Briony rounded on him. "You had no right to do such a thing to me."

"I beg your pardon!"

"How dare you spring it on me without warning!"

"Spring what?"

"Deirdre Raye—oh, no, it's Grant now that she's *free*, as she made a point of telling me."

"I didn't spring her on you. We discussed her and I told you there was nothing in it."

"Yes, you did. And I believed you. More fool me!"

"Are you calling me a liar?" he asked quietly.

"I don't know what to call you. Why did you pretend there'd never been anything between you and Deirdre?"

"I didn't pretend. It was the truth."

"Don't treat me like a fool—"

"You *are* calling me a liar."

She turned on him, eyes flashing. "Put it any way you like. I don't care what women you've had. Why should I? It's none of my business. But why not be open with me?"

Carlyle shook his head as if trying to clear it. "Shall I go out and come in again? So far I haven't followed any of this."

"I don't like being made a fool of. I felt so stupid when she said it—well, implied it."

"Well, if she only implied it, that's all right, isn't it? Now all you have to do is tell me what she implied and we might be getting somewhere."

"She flaunted those rubies under my nose and talked about how you always knew the right jewels to give a woman. You should have prepared me for it, that's all." Briony realized that he was looking at her in fascination. "You're not going to deny that you gave them to her, are you?"

"No, I don't deny it."

"Well—that's that, then."

Carlyle was staring at her. Suddenly he gave a crack of laughter, sat on the bed and dropped his head into his hands, his shoulders shaking.

"What's so funny?" Briony seethed.

"You are. Oh, lord!"

"I'm glad I've given you a good laugh."

He pulled himself together. "I'm sorry. I should have listened to you when you said Deirdre had me in her sights. How was I to know she'd read so much into a friendly gesture?"

"Several thousand pounds' worth of rubies and gold is a friendly gesture?" she demanded scathingly. "Who are you? Midas?"

"I was feeling like Midas the night I made her that gift. George, her husband, had just put me in the way of making a lot of money in a short time. The three of us went out to dinner to celebrate, and I gave her a thank-you gift."

"Oh, really? If *he'd* done you the favor, why give *her* rubies?"

"I'd have looked a fool giving them to him, wouldn't I?"

"You know what I mean."

"I repaid George in ways that a businessman would appreciate. The rubies were a graceful compliment to the wife of my benefactor. I even consulted George about what she'd like, and I gave them to her in front of him. I told you the truth. There was never anything between me and Deirdre—except, it seems, in her mind. I'm grateful for the way you dealt with her. I could never have done it so effectively." He eyed her, amused. "What *did* you call her, by the way?"

"Never mind."

"All right." He grinned and added wickedly, "I'll ask Emma."

"I don't think you should encourage the child to repeat something I should never have said."

"Don't spoil it by having a conscience," he begged. "I was impressed."

"All right. I said she was devious."

"Is that all?"

Briony shrugged. "I may also have said scheming, two-faced and spiteful."

"You've really got your knife into her, haven't you?" He grinned. "With anyone but my cool, steady Briony, I'd suspect jealousy."

It was like a match thrown into straw. Eyes flashing, Briony whirled on him. "How dare you say that!" she blazed. "How *dare* you! My only concern is Emma."

He looked astonished. "All right. I'm sorry."

"Everything I do is for Emma," she seethed, "and I think it was unforgivable the way that woman insinuated things about you and her in a way that Emma could have found very upsetting."

"Upsetting, my foot!" Carlyle said, torn between exasperation and amusement. "Our daughter was the only one who finished the evening with a smile on her face."

"Because I dealt with Deirdre for her, which you should have done."

"I would have if you hadn't managed so splendidly. I was thinking that I hope I never get on your wrong side, but I seem to be on it anyway."

"You shouldn't have made that remark about jealousy. It was cheap."

"Stop bawling me out, you little shrew. It was only a harmless joke."

"A joke in very poor taste," Briony snapped. Her nerves were in tatters, and all the repressed emotions of the last few weeks were overflowing. She wheeled away from him, trying to use up some of the nervous energy that infused her before her unruly tongue pitched her into disaster.

Carlyle stared at her. "Lord, I never knew you had such a temper. I'm still not entirely sure what I did."

She nearly screamed at him, *You talked to her, you laughed with her and gave her rubies. She knew you when I didn't.*

The temptation to say it was so strong that she was shaken with the awareness of danger. This must stop before it was too late. "I don't think we should say any more," she declared primly. "I'm tired. I want to go to bed."

"Oh, really?" he enquired with a touch of grim hilarity. "Suppose I want to go on fighting?"

"We're not fighting."

"You could have fooled me."

"*We are not fighting!* There's nothing more to say. You've cleared up the problem."

"Then why do I get the feeling that you're still mad at me? Briony, if there's something troubling you, let's have it out in the open."

"I've told you what was troubling me—"

"No, there's something more, something you're keeping to yourself." He seized her arms and held her steady. "Stop storming about the room like an agitated wasp, and talk to me properly. Briony, do you dislike me?"

"Do I—what?"

"I've begun to think that you must. There's some seething undercurrent in your attitude to me. You're tense. You won't let me get near you. The other night when I dared to—well, I can't blame you for that. I was out of line. But tonight, just because I made that little joke about jealousy, you turn on me as if you hated me. Do you?"

"Of course not," she stammered. "Let me go, Carlyle. Everything's all right. I was being silly—"

"No, let's talk about this."

She tried to pull away from him but Carlyle held on. In the short scuffle that followed Briony found the long hem of her nightdress under her feet. She staggered, caught the other foot in the material and fell against Carlyle. His hands tightened, steadying her.

His pajama jacket had fallen open, revealing his smooth bare chest. The little bow on her nightdress had come undone, allowing the edges to fall apart, uncovering her breasts, rising and falling in her agitation. The touch of his warm skin against her own sent shock waves through her. She tried to control them but her whole being was thrumming with the excitement of anger, and this new thrill heightened her sensations. She was sharply conscious of Carlyle's face looking down at her, his lips parted, his breath coming raggedly. She didn't know that her cheeks were flushed and her eyes blazing as he'd never seen them before. She only knew that his face held a look of pure astonishment. It was the last thing she saw before he bent his head and smothered her mouth with his own.

Passion, fierce and hot, surged up in her. Last time he'd kissed her she'd been sensible about it, but no power on earth could have made her sensible now. She wanted to embrace him with all her strength, but she couldn't do that because he was holding her so tightly. His hands gripped her arms, making it impossible for her to move them, while his lips moved purposefully, insistently over hers. She thrilled at the determination with which he held her. This was no actor in a bloodless bargain, but a man in the grip of feelings stronger than himself. Briony's senses rioted and she pressed close to him, longing for him to lose all restraint.

"Carlyle..." she gasped.

"You shouldn't look at me like that, Briony," he said against her mouth. "It isn't safe..."

She didn't want to be safe. She wanted to be lost with him in mutual passion, but before she could tell him, he was sliding his arms round her, imprisoning her more firmly, while he explored her mouth.

"Beautiful," he murmured, "driving me crazy..."

"Yes—yes—" she gasped. What she'd longed for was about to happen. In another moment...

She felt a shudder go through his powerful frame. The next moment he pushed her away. She could feel him trembling violently. "No," he said. *"No!"*

"Carlyle—" The word came out as a ragged gasp.

He put a distance between them. "It's not all my fault this time," he said. "You're enticing enough to tempt any man to forget his principles. I've never seen you like this before—" He ran a hand distractedly through his hair. "And it's all because you're mad at me. I should have remembered that."

She looked at him, dazed at how quickly the dream had been snatched away. "What are you saying?"

"I'm saying that I want you—right this minute I want you more than I've ever—but I'm in control of it. Don't look at me like that. You can trust me. It's a passing mood, and it'll—pass. I'm just sorry that I forgot how you felt."

"You don't know how I feel," she cried in anguish.

"I think I do. You've made it pretty plain. We're neither of us the sort of person that gives in to a moment's madness."

"Aren't we? Do you find it easy to be so wise?"

"No, I don't find it easy at all. I wish I'd never seen you this way."

"But you have seen me," she said desperately. "And you wanted me. Maybe sometimes—you should just stop being so controlled and just—do what you want."

"And have you hate me afterward?"

"I could never hate you, Carlyle."

His breathing was calmer now. "No, you're too kind for that. I was forgetting what a mountain of debt I already owe your kindness. I'm a taker, Briony, you know that. I've never been ashamed of it before, but I am now. For a moment I wanted you so much I'd have taken you and hang the consequences. But in the morning..."

"Yes," she said dully. "In the morning..."

In the morning he would have flinched away from her, and their relationship would have become impossible.

Carlyle began to pull on his dressing gown. "Don't worry," he said. "I'm going to sleep on the sofa in my study."

"Suppose Emma finds out?" Briony said automatically. The words steadied her, reminding her why she was here.

"I'll set the alarm early and come back here for an hour. That's if you don't mind."

She gave a brief laugh. "No," she said bleakly. "I don't mind."

"Thank you. I'll get out of your way now." He vanished quickly.

Briony threw herself on the bed and lay there, dry-eyed, trying to quieten the tumult in her flesh and the worse tumult in her heart. She'd come so close to finding a way through to him, but he'd backed off for fear of too much involvement. And that was how it would always be.

CHAPTER EIGHT

AFTER the events of that night Briony had feared to find some constraint between them, and it seemed to her that she saw less of Carlyle for a couple of days. But then Emma caught a severe cold, and in the alarm that followed they forgot about themselves. The doctor was reassuring, insisting that she was holding up well, but she was confined to bed for several days, feverish and miserable. Carlyle immediately switched his work to home, visiting Emma regularly, but then retreating to his study and the safety of the computer screen.

"Couldn't you stay a little longer and talk to her?" Briony protested one night as they prepared for bed. They could act naturally with each other now.

He sighed. "I keep meaning to, but I don't know what to say. I played Snakes and Ladders with her all this afternoon."

"Yes, but afterward she wanted to chat about the ballet she'd seen on television, and you just handed her over to me and escaped."

"You can talk about ballet much better than I can," he said defensively. "Look, when she's better I'll take you both to whatever you want. Will that do?"

"Only if you take an interest and talk to her about it afterward."

Carlyle dropped his head in his hands. "We've been through this before," he groaned. "I'm doing my best. It's just that when it comes to words I—"

"I know words are hard for you," she said more gently. "But the words are often what she wants. Buying her things is easy. Even when she wanted a mother, The Great Fixer just went out and arranged it, like a business deal. But she might not have missed a mother so much if she'd had a father who was there more."

"I give her my time," he said furiously. "You can't say I don't."

"But how much of that time do you spend *alone* with her, talking one-to-one about what she wants to talk about? The day I met Emma you were taking her to the funfair with Tom—"

"I needed Tom to drop us off near the fair and save Emma the walk," he defended himself quickly.

"But you added me to the party fast enough, didn't you? I wondered about that then, but I see why now."

He sighed. "Well, what would you have me talk to her about?" he asked. "Shall I tell her all the things I'm thinking and feeling? Don't you realize that sometimes I'm afraid to talk to my child, for fear of what I might let slip?"

She touched his arm gently. "I'm sorry. I know you do your best."

"But it's not enough," he said morosely. "Do you think I don't know that? Don't blame me too much, Briony. There are things you can't understand."

She was silent for a moment before saying slowly, "Perhaps I understand better than you think."

"I know you love Emma, but you only met her a few months ago. Can you imagine losing a child who's been a part of your life for years? Of course you can't."

She looked at him. "I don't have to imagine. I know."

Something in her manner caught his attention. He searched her face. "What are you saying? I thought you'd never had a child."

"I had a little sister. I raised her after our parents died. She was full of life and mischief until—" Briony stopped as she was invaded by memories.

Carlyle took hold of her gently. "Tell me what happened," he said.

"She became poorly. I thought it was just a cold, but she got worse quickly, and when I called the doctor he said it was meningitis. They fought so hard to save her at the hospital—but it was too late. She was eight years old."

"When did all this happen?" he asked.

"January this year."

"Just a few months ago!" he exclaimed, aghast. "My God! Why didn't you tell me before?"

"I meant to—at first—when you wanted me to be here for Emma," she said haltingly. "I was going refuse, but Emma needed me so much. I did my best not to brood about Sally but—" A tremor went through her as her grief poured out. "I loved her so much, and I failed her—"

"Don't say that," Carlyle interrupted quickly. "It wasn't your fault."

"I've tried to tell myself that, but she's dead and I could have saved her if I'd acted quicker."

"You don't know that. It might have been too late anyway, and meningitis is very hard to spot at first—"

"But she's dead," Briony said desperately. "She's *dead*. Nothing's going to change that." Tears poured down her face. "It's so final and irrevocable—no one else can know—"

"That's true," he said quietly, taking her into his arms. "No one else can know what we know. Don't cry, Briony."

"I can't help it," she choked. A violent trembling had seized her. She wept for Sally, for Emma, for the pain of the man she loved, and the bleakness of her own life when she would have lost him.

He drew her closer, soothing her with murmured words, stroking her hair, her face, trying to reach through her grief and console her. Briony felt his tenderness enfolding her, and she relaxed in his arms, feeling that she'd found safety at last. For the first time, here was someone she could cling to, who would be strong for her. Only half realizing what she was doing, she put her arms about him, silently pleading for she knew not what. She wanted him in every way, as husband, lover and friend. It might all be no more than an illusion, but just now she would settle for the illusion if only she could be close to him.

She felt his kisses fall on her lips, her eyes, her face. "Don't cry, my dear," he murmured. "I'm here—I'm here."

"Yes," she murmured huskily. "I'm so glad you're here. Stay with me—hold me—I've been alone so much. I don't want to be alone anymore."

He silenced her by gently caressing her mouth with his own. His arms about her had the power of steel, but there was only tenderness in his lips. Something gave way inside her. She'd held out against her desire, but she had no resistance to the tide of sweetness that flooded her at his loving compassion. Her body was pressed against his so closely that she could feel his heart beating. Her own was pounding strongly, hopefully.

His hands moved cautiously over her, touching the swell of her breasts, her waist, her hips.

"Briony..." he murmured.

"Hush—don't say anything."

"But are you sure? I thought you—"

She touched his mouth with her fingertips before he could say more. Words would only spoil the magic. And besides, what could she say to him? That she was sure and not sure, at the same time? That she was doing something she knew would break her heart, but she would pay the price if only she might have this moment? None of this could be put into words. So she spoke to him silently, with the eagerness of her lips, and the willingness of her body, and thrilled as she felt him respond with ardor.

His kiss changed, became deeper, more searching. The tip of his tongue flickered over the silky inside of her mouth. Tremors of pleasure began to course through her, until her whole body was heated with delight. She felt alive, as though every nerve glittered. She belonged to him heart and soul, and for a brief spell she could dream that he belonged to her.

The last of her sadness fell away as his lips began to trace a line down her neck, lingering at her throat where a little pulse beat madly, surely telling him of her desire. She gave a long sigh of heated anticipation as she felt him begin to remove her nightdress. His own nightclothes joined hers on the floor. She'd dreamed of lying naked with him, but the reality was far sweeter than her dreams. His body was hard and warm, pressed against hers in gentle intimacy. He touched her carefully at first, caressing her breasts with his fingertips, his lips, his tongue.

Warmth was streaming through her. Love and desire mingled so perfectly that she couldn't tell where emotion ended and sensation began. She only knew that each was a part of her response to this man, and each needed the other. When he moved over her she was ready for him, welcoming him gladly, feeling herself made complete at last by their union.

She whispered his name, looking up into his face, close to hers. In the dim light she could just discern his smile, his look of tenderness. She embraced him, drawing him near, running her hands down the long, springy line of his back to the lean hips. Everything about him made her rejoice, the nutty, masculine smell of his body, the smoothness of his skin, the power of his loins, driving her to heights of pleasure, so that she seemed to stand on the pinnacle of the world, and everything was beautiful.

She came back to earth slowly, held safe by his arms. "Carlyle," she murmured.

"Hush." He silenced her with a kiss, and turned, still holding her so that her head rested on his shoulder. "Hush now—hush."

Lying in the darkness, Briony heard Carlyle's voice over her head. "You're very quiet. Are you asleep?"

"No," she whispered. "I dozed a little, but I'm awake now."

She'd been thinking happily about the tumultuous events of the past hour. To be loved by Carlyle, to feel her body achieve heights of ecstasy in his arms, and to drift off to sleep held safe in his embrace; this was more joy than she had dared to hope for. But it had all happened. And now she was wondering what it meant. Had his feelings warmed toward her? Could a man make love to a woman with such passion and tenderness without loving her a little, in his heart? His next words would tell her.

"Are you angry with me?" he asked.

"No. Why should I be angry?"

"Because I broke my word. I tried not to but—I'm so grateful for all your kindness. And for once you seemed to need a little kindness, too. I guess I got carried away. As long as you don't mind..."

"No," she said with a little sigh. "I don't mind." She was silent a moment as her hopes died. "After all—" she gave an awkward little laugh "—we are married—kind of. And...and we need each other's help in all sorts of ways."

"Yes," he agreed in a voice that she was sure held relief. "No strings, no ties. Just two loving friends helping each other over the thorny places."

"Yes," she said.

She lay still, wondering if he would speak again, but he didn't. After a while she dozed, and when she woke it was to find him missing. She crept out onto the landing and looked downstairs. His study door was standing open. Moving down a few more stairs, she saw Carlyle, sitting at his desk, staring at the picture of Helen cradling the newborn Emma. In his other hand he held the wedding photo of Emma walking with Briony through the leaves. He was looking from one to the other, as if in a dream. Then he set both pictures down and buried his head in his hands.

Briony returned to bed with a heavy heart.

She discovered, however, that one good thing had come out of that night. When Emma found her looking at photographs of Sally, and asked her about them, she was able to talk about her sister naturally. Emma nodded and said nothing, but she put her arms about Briony and gave her a sympathetic hug. Carlyle came in to find them going through the pictures together.

Later, when they were alone, he said, "You should have talked about Sally before, not kept it hidden. It hurts more that way."

"Yes, I guess you know that, too," she agreed. "I didn't want Emma to feel she had to share me. But it *has* hurt, hiding Sally away."

"She looks fun," Carlyle observed.

"Oh, yes, she was great fun," Briony said eagerly. "She was full of mischief. Look at this one—"

She pointed to a picture showing Sally dressed as a conjurer, standing before a Christmas tree. "I gave her that conjuring set," Briony remembered. "And she went round casting 'spells' on everyone."

"What is it?" Carlyle asked, seeing a shadow cross her face.

"She wanted a bike for Christmas," Briony said sadly. "I told her it was more than I could afford. She was disappointed, but so nice about it. She smiled and said, 'Maybe next year.' And I promised." Briony's voice grew husky. "If I'd known that she only had a few weeks left to live I'd have got her that bike somehow." She sighed. "It's nearly Christmas again."

"Oh, God!" Carlyle said softly. "Emma."

"Yes. We've got to make this the best Christmas she's ever had. It doesn't matter about us."

He nodded. "Once I would have wondered where I'd get the strength. Now I know I'll get it from you. But you—where do you get yours from?"

From my love for you, she told him in the silence of her heart. I didn't know before how love gives you the strength to do anything you have to do. But I know it now.

* * *

Emma was very definite about what she wanted for Christmas. "Dancing classes, please. I used to go, until I was ill, but I'm better now."

"Not yet," Carlyle said. "Wait until you're a little stronger. Anyway, dancing classes wouldn't fit into your Christmas stocking."

"Yes they would," Emma said. "Father Christmas would find a way. He can do anything."

"But *I* can't," Carlyle said.

"It wouldn't be you. It would be Father Christmas," Emma pointed out.

"But—" Carlyle broke off, looking puzzled. "What's all this Father Christmas talk? Last year you said you didn't believe in him."

"No, I didn't."

"You did. I remember."

Emma's eyes were wide and innocent. "No, I didn't, Daddy."

Carlyle caught Briony's warning eyes on him and backtracked hastily. "I must have got it wrong."

"Father Christmas comes through the landing window because we haven't got a chimney," Emma recited. "I saw him once. Don't you remember?"

To Briony's amusement Carlyle looked suddenly awkward. "Yes—yes, I do."

Briony waited until Emma was in bed before asking, "What's going on? Who did she see coming in the window?"

"Me. My mother made me dress up for a few years, but I gave it up when Emma stopped believing."

"But she hasn't stopped believing."

"I swear to you that last year Emma—oh, well, it doesn't matter now."

"Where's the costume?"

"In the attic somewhere."

"I'll get it down and clean it."

Carlyle looked harassed. "Whatever made her suddenly go back to believing in Father Christmas?"

Briony thought she could have told him, but judged it wiser to keep her own counsel.

One evening when Emma was in bed she climbed into the attic to search for Santa's robe. It was a hard task because the attic light didn't work. She borrowed Carlyle's car torch with the neon strip down the side and propped it up on a box while she studied the dusty attic. After an hour of clambering about, unpacking boxes and achieving nothing, she was hot, dusty and irritable.

"What are you doing?" Carlyle's head appeared through the floor.

"Trying to find your Santa costume," she told him fretfully. "But I don't think it's here. You must have remembered it wrong."

"No, I didn't. I know it's up here somewhere."

"Well, where is it, then?" she demanded crossly. "I'm fed up with looking."

In the half light she could see him grin. "You've got a smudge on your nose."

"I feel smudged all over." She made vague, ineffectual attempts to brush herself down, and he joined in.

"Now I'm smudged," he said after a moment.

"Good. Then you won't mind getting even dirtier finding that cloak for me," Briony observed.

"If I remember rightly it's in that suitcase over there."

"You mean the one at the bottom of everything else?" she said faintly.

"That's the one." Meeting hostility in her eyes he said, "Well, since I'm already in a mess—" He made his way gingerly over to a heap by the wall, and, after some grunting, managed to extract the suitcase without bringing everything down on top of him. When he'd hauled it over and got it open they found that his memory had served him well. An ancient Father Christmas robe was folded inside. It was the old-fashioned kind with voluminous skirts that swept the floor. Briony regarded it with delight.

"Fancy you buying a thing like this," she said.

"Helen bought it while she was carrying Emma. She had it all planned that I was going to wear it the first Christmas after the baby was born." He sighed. "Well—that didn't happen."

"What was Helen like?" Briony asked.

He seemed to become awkward. "Pretty," he said at last. "The same way Emma is. Helen was mad about ballet, too. She wanted to be a dancer, but she gave it up to marry me. She was like that. She always made me feel I came first. She transformed my life..."

He was staring into the distance. Briony watched his eyes grow soft with memory, and wondered what was the matter with her that she tormented herself like this. Obviously Carlyle had never got over Helen's death. He valued Briony's friendship, and sometimes he desired her, but it was Helen that he loved.

"I'm glad you made me do this," he said at last, looking down at the red and white robe.

"It's what she'd have wanted you to do."

"You know everything." He smiled at her. "You understand Emma and me, and you get everything right by instinct. I think Helen would have liked you. Thank you, Briony, with all my heart." He took her hand in his. "I hope this Christmas won't be too hard on you, remembering Sally."

Impulsively she said, "I can cope with Sally's memory now. No one can go on looking back forever. The past has to become the past, Carlyle. We have to be strong enough to let it." She stopped. She could hear the note of dangerous intensity in her own voice, a subtle pleading for him to give the past to Helen and the future to herself.

He frowned, and she wondered if he'd detected her underlying meaning. But if he had, it displeased him. He gave a brief, uneasy smile and dropped her hand.

"I'm afraid this robe has got pretty dirty up here," he said lightly.

"Don't worry. I've got plenty of time to get it clean."

"Fine. Well, let's get on, then."

They left the attic together.

The week before Christmas Carlyle and Tom put up a huge tree in the garden, and hung it with lights. Emma watched, shining-eyed, from the window.

"Do you think it will snow?" she asked Briony for the hundredth time. "I love snow."

"Then it'll snow," she promised, hoping that Emma's last Christmas would be made perfect in every way.

She festooned the house with garlands, red and gold, blue, green and silver. Then there was another tree in the big room downstairs, hung with fairy lights that winked on and off, their reflections gleaming in the baubles that hung from each branch.

Day followed day without snow. There was the rush of shopping, buying in the mountain of food that would be needed for all the guests, choosing presents. Emma pondered long over Carlyle's gift, turning the pages of the catalogue Briony had brought from the store to save her having to make tiring journeys.

"What about that?" she said, pointing to an elegant leather dressing case. "Daddy's always going on trips abroad to sell things to people."

"I hadn't noticed."

"Well, he stopped when I wasn't well. But I expect he'll be going again soon now I'm better."

"Let's get him that, then."

"What do you want for Christmas, Mummy?"

"I don't know. I haven't thought."

"But you must," Emma said earnestly. "I have to tell Daddy." At once a guilty look came over her face and she clapped a hand over her mouth. "I wasn't supposed to tell you that."

Briony chuckled. "So you've been sent to spy out the land? All right. I'll do some serious thinking."

Mentally she applauded Carlyle, who'd remembered her advice about drawing Emma into a benign conspiracy. She couldn't tell Emma that what she really wanted for Christmas was Carlyle's love, gift-wrapped for the occasion; she told her that she was fond of musical shows, and her collection still had some gaps. Emma noted down the recordings Briony already possessed, and went away looking solemn with responsibility.

Carlyle was everywhere with his camera these days, picturing Emma stirring the Christmas pudding, for Nora made her own. Emma in the choir for the school's Christmas concert. Emma wrapping gifts and writing labels, her tongue stuck out with concentration; Emma joining a crowd of carol singers who called one night and sang around the tree in the garden. That one was especially hard to watch, with the lights falling on her eager, upturned face and shining eyes, her childish voice raised in Christmas worship for the last time.

"Let's put them away," Carlyle said, turning off the video. "Next year will be the time to watch them."

They were sitting in the near darkness at one in the morning. Briony could hardly see him, but she could sense the outlines of his body, drained and weary with the effort of putting on a smiling face while his heart broke.

"Let's go to bed," she said, touching him gently.

"Yes, all ri— Good God! What's that?"

From up above them came the sound of Emma's voice calling urgently. "Mummy, Daddy! Come quick."

"She's ill," he said in fear. "She's had a bad turn."

They rushed out into the hall to be confronted by Emma's nightgowned figure on the landing, bouncing with excitement.

"Come and look!" she cried urgently, pointing out of the window. "It's *snowing*."

CHAPTER NINE

AT THE wedding Briony had had little time to take in the details of Carlyle's family, but when they arrived for Christmas she began to observe them more closely. Joyce was as she'd remembered, warm-hearted and bracing, with a tendency to sweep all before her. It amused Briony to realize that just as Emma had inherited her forceful strain from Carlyle, so he'd inherited it from his mother.

Lionel, his father, was a mild man, a few inches shorter than his wife, who regarded the world with an air of bemusement, and his son with something like awe. He had no business sense himself, and left all household paperwork to his wife. His own interest was painting, and he arrived with an easel and palette and promptly set to work in the garden, trying to capture the falling snow, until Joyce hauled him indoors with a trenchant demand to know if he'd set his heart on pneumonia, or would he be satisfied with flu?

Apart from them there was Carlyle's older sister Paula, who held a tutorship at a university some distance away. She was a tense woman with a stern aspect and a sarcastic tongue. But Briony noticed that Emma liked her and would seek her company, ignoring snubs, or perhaps not feeling them as snubs.

The younger sister, Elaine, had come up from Cornwall with her husband and eleven-year-old twins, Dawn and Belinda. They were jolly children, but sensible, and both of them obviously knew that they had to treat Emma with care. After the first hour Briony left the three of them together with an easy mind.

The day before Christmas Eve she was still making charts and lists to find ways to accommodate so many guests. She managed it at last, and although the house nearly burst at the seams, at least everyone had a bed. And even Paula declared that there was something cheerful about so many people under one roof.

"Not that you'll think so on Christmas Day, when the rest arrive," she declared gloomily.

"Are there many more?" Briony asked. "I knew at one time, but I've lost track."

"Various cousins," Paula declared, dismissing them with a wave of her hand. Denis—you met him at the wedding. Peter, Andrew—they're all right, some of them. At least Peter isn't such a fool as he looks. Not like Denis, who *is*."

Emma giggled.

"Well, I know you like him," Paula said. "All children do. Mind of a child himself, if you ask me."

"Exactly," Carlyle said with some asperity. "I don't remember inviting him for Christmas. If fact, I don't remember inviting him to our wedding."

"Of course not," Joyce agreed. "Nobody invites Denis anywhere. It isn't necessary. He simply turns up."

Somehow, in the melee, Briony got a chance for a quiet sherry in the kitchen with Joyce. Now they were friends it was easy to confide her worries about Carlyle's inability to talk to Emma, except superficially.

"He adores her, he'd do anything, give anything—except speak to her from his heart. At first I thought it was wonderful that he could play the 'Oswald' game, until I realized that the Oswalds make it easy for him. While he's fooling about them he doesn't have to be talking about anything else. He's not a shallow man—"

"Oh, no, quite the reverse," Joyce said. "Things go so deep with him that he can't find the words. It's the same with his father. The only way Lionel can talk is through paint. He's never told me that he loves me, but all his best portraits of me have been done since I lost my youthful looks. That's how I know."

Briony smiled. "That's nice. But I wasn't talking about Carlyle and me."

"If your husband can't speak of his feelings, it must be your problem, too," Joyce said shrewdly.

A jealous imp made Briony ask, "How did Helen manage? Did he tell her he loved her?"

"I'm not sure. But that was different. You see, they grew up next door to each other, went to school together, understood each other through and through. Helen didn't need the words."

"I see," Briony said with a sigh. "Yes, I see."

On Christmas Eve Emma said anxiously, "Daddy, you forgot the ladder."

"What ladder?"

"The one to the landing window, for Father Christmas."

"He doesn't need a ladder, darling. The reindeer will drop him just outside."

"He's always needed a ladder before. You used to put it up against the wall and leave the window open six inches."

Carlyle gave in without further argument. "All right. A ladder."

Lionel helped him carry it from the shed, and Briony stood and watched as the two of them adjusted it.

"There," she said. "Now Father Christmas can get in without any trouble."

Her husband cast her a disgruntled glance. "As far as I'm concerned," he muttered, "Father Christmas can fall down it and—"

"Careful. Emma's at the window. *Is that all right, darling?*"

"Perfect," Emma called back.

"Time for bed."

It was easier to get Emma to bed now she was sharing her room with Dawn and Belinda. The whispering went on far into the night, as Briony had discovered, listening outside. Tonight she watched as they hung up their stockings, and mentally ran over the plan. The three children would be allowed out when the church clock struck midnight, which would just be in time to see Father Christmas's arrival. He would go downstairs to put the main presents around the tree, and while the children watched this Joyce would slip into their rooms and exchange the empty stockings for identical ones filled with oranges and small toys.

At eleven-thirty, when the house was growing quiet, Carlyle asked, "Just how far do I have to take this? Because if you think that I'm going to climb in through that window—"

"No, of course not," Briony soothed him. "You can't actually see the window from the spot where Emma will be watching, so she won't know how you got into position. Come on. You've come this far. Don't give up now."

"You will make sure that Emma's watching, won't you? I'd hate to think I was making a fool of myself for nothing."

"Leave it to me."

At ten minutes to midnight Briony checked the landing outside Emma's room. It was empty, but a cheeky head appeared around her door. "Midnight, and not a moment before," Briony told her. "Back now."

The head obediently vanished. Briony went down to Carlyle. "The coast's clear. Quick."

Together they went to the little junk room near the window, where she'd stored the costume. After helping him on with it, she said, "Now, you've just come in through that window, with your sack full of presents. You creep out onto the landing and look around you. Then you go downstairs and in the hall you discover the beer and mince pie that Emma's left you, and you look delighted."

"How can I look delighted under this hood?"

"You can give a big thumbs-up sign. Make sure you're near the little wall light, so that she can get a good view. She'll be looking through the banisters. Then you go into the front room and put the presents around the tree. As you come back you drink the beer, eat the mince pie. Now you're almost ready to go."

The window through which Santa was supposed to climb had been left open a few inches on the insistence of Emma, who plainly had the poorest opinion of his ability to get in without help. Briony now pulled aside the heavy curtains, meaning to fasten it shut, and gave a little gasp. Before her incredulous gaze, the window was being pulled wide open. A hand appeared.

"Someone's breaking in," Carlyle murmured.

"Perhaps it's Father Christmas," she said light-headedly.

"Nonsense. How can it be Father Christmas when *I*—" Carlyle checked himself on the verge of an absurdity, and heard Briony smother a laugh.

"Wait here," he said masterfully, and launched himself forward just as someone came over the sill.

What happened next didn't take long. There was a thump as they hit the floor together, followed by a scuffle that ended with Father Christmas on top.

"Ow! Gerroff!" said a familiar voice.

"Denis!" they both said together.

"What the devil are you doing breaking into my house?" Carlyle demanded.

"No such thing. I just arrived a little early. I thought I'd slide in quietly, so as not to cause any trouble, and was attacked by a mad Santa."

Briony hastily closed the window. "Get up, you two," she said. "The clock's striking twelve."

Carlyle rose and took up his sack.

"You? Father Christmas?" Denis demanded. "Let me do it."

"Definitely not," Carlyle growled from behind his beard.

"It's the sort of thing I'd do much better than you, you know I would. Come on, let me—"

Denis had started to pull at the heavy white beard. The next minute he was startled to find himself pinned against the wall, with a pair of blazing eyes staring straight into his own.

"Get this straight," Santa raged. "There's only one person going to be Father Christmas to my daughter, and that's me. Do I make myself quite clear?"

"All right, all right," Denis said in a strangled voice.

"Any more trouble from you and you'll find yourself back out in the snow." Santa released his prey, who slid down the wall rubbing his throat and breathing hard.

From overhead, out of sight, came the sound of childish whispers. "Never mind this now," Briony urged. "You've got a job to do."

Carlyle hoisted the sack on his shoulders and went along the passage to the landing, where he began to descend the stairs into the dimly lit hall. Briony moved quietly behind him until she could see the stairwell, and the faces of three children overhead, watching everything intently. They were perfectly still as Father Christmas reached the hall, but when he gave a big thumbs-up sign over the refreshments smiles broke out all over their faces, and they began to creep down further.

From their new vantage point they saw him approach the tree, covered with glittering lights and tinsel, and begin to empty his sack around the base, laying gifts to right and left with great care. The job finished, he crept out of the room to where the refreshments waited.

As he drank the beer Briony saw one child detach herself from the others and move softly down the stairs. At last Father Christmas finished the mince pie, but before he could move, a small figure came flying off the last step and launched herself at him. Santa clasped her tight, her little face buried beneath his billowing beard, and the two of them stayed like that for a long time.

Later, in bed, Carlyle said wonderingly, "She knew it was me from the start, didn't she?"

"Of course she did," Briony said, smiling. "She told you last year, she doesn't believe in Father Christmas anymore."

"Then why pretend that she did?"

"Work it out."

After a moment he said, "Yes—I understand. At least—I think so. The little monkey wanted to see if she could make me jump through hoops for her, didn't she?"

"Yes, and you did," she told him tenderly. "You jumped through them beautifully."

Denis spent the night on the sofa near the tree. "Guarding the presents," he said cheerily. "Santa's Little Helper."

Next morning, as the house was stirring, he went around decorating everywhere with mistletoe, of which he seemed to have brought a liberal supply.

The children were bouncing with excitement, eager to open the presents. The grown-ups gathered around the tree, and the ceremony began.

Emma was overwhelmed by her gifts. Briony had bought everything to delight a little dancer's heart, practice tunic, tights and shoes, plus a pink satin tutu, and a pair of "best" dancing shoes. Emma promptly darted upstairs and returned clad in the tutu and tights. She curtsied to general applause and announced her intention of dressing like this all day. There was an ache in Briony's heart but she smiled. Emma could dream, and need never know that the dream couldn't come true.

When the children had strewn the room with brightly colored wrapping paper, the adults could turn to their own gifts. Briony had two shocks. Instead of the modest few recordings she'd asked for, Carlyle and Emma presented her with state-of-the-art CD equipment, and versions of just about every musical and operetta written.

Her second shock was another set of gifts and cards. "Happy birthday," Carlyle said, giving them to her.

"But how did you know my birthday was at Christmas?" she asked in delight.

Carlyle and his daughter exchanged grins. "Put it there," he said, crooking his little finger, and Emma curled her own little finger round it. Solemnly they shook.

"A little nifty liaison work," he said. "I briefed my agent in the field here to discover your birthday."

"I found your birth certificate," Emma said.

"And passed the information on to me," Carlyle added. "When we realized your birthday fell on Christmas Day we decided to surprise you."

"It's the best surprise I ever had," she said. But the greatest pleasure of all was the fact that he could have discovered her birthday from her work records. Instead he'd consulted Emma.

A piece of Denis's mistletoe hung directly overhead. It would have been so easy for Carlyle to make use of it, but apparently it didn't occur to him. He squeezed her shoulder kindly, said, "As long as you're pleased," and the moment passed.

The house seethed and hummed with people. Not until supper was over did Briony snatch a moment alone. She escaped to the kitchen, in dire need of a cup of tea. Suddenly she was depressed. The day was nearly over, and Carlyle had ignored the mistletoe. With a sigh, she contemplated the washing up.

"Don't worry, I've promised Nora I'll do it," said a cheery voice.

"Hello, Denis. Don't tell me the party got too much for you, too? You were born to make a party go with a swing."

He fanned himself. "Even the court jester needs five minutes off. Is that tea you're making?"

"Yes. Coming up in just a minute."

While she busied herself making tea she was vaguely aware that Denis was reaching over her head, but she had no idea what he was doing until she looked round for the milk and found him regarding her with an impish look.

"What are you up to, Denis?"

"D'you see what's up there?" he enquired innocently.

Briony looked up to the light, where Denis had stuck another piece of mistletoe to the metal shade. Before she could stop him he'd put both arms around her and kissed her full on the lips.

She wasn't pleased, but neither was she annoyed. It was only Denis acting the fool. "That's enough," she said, laughing and trying to free her arms, which he'd imprisoned. "Let me go now."

"You wouldn't begrudge me one little Christmas kiss, would you?"

"You've had it."

"How about another?"

"Denis, I'm warning you—"

"Ah, don't be heartless, Briony. I've fancied you like mad ever since I met you at the wedding, and Christmas only comes once a year. Be kind to a starving man."

"Starving my foot, you had half the turkey."

"Starving for love. Famished for affection. One touch of your ruby lips and I'll live on it for a year."

Briony freed herself and seized up the soup ladle. "You won't survive five minutes if I use this on you," she warned.

"She spurns me! Calamity!" Denis released her and struck his forehead, seemingly about to expire with grief. Briony chuckled at his clowning and put down the ladle.

It was a mistake. Quick as a flash Denis flung an arm around her shoulders and drew her close to seize another kiss. Briony, caught off balance, fended him off clumsily. Then, as suddenly as he'd pounced on her, he vanished. She had a glimpse of Carlyle's face, tight with anger. She steadied herself in time to see Denis being irresistibly propelled out of the kitchen. They vanished into the hall, from where Briony heard muffled voices. Denis saying placatingly, "Don't be hard on Santa's Little Helper." And Carlyle, not at all placated, snapping, "Santa's Little Helper is lucky he doesn't find himself strung up on the tree."

"Thank you," she said when Carlyle returned. "He was getting a bit much to handle."

"Indeed? A wise woman wouldn't have come out here alone with him," Carlyle said coldly.

She looked up and found him regarding her darkly. "Hey, come on," she said. "I didn't 'come out here' with him. I came out alone for a cuppa and a bit of peace, and he followed."

"With one aim."

"Well, don't blame me for that. Don't make so much of it. It's just fooling."

"So you say."

"Well, you don't seriously think it was anything else, do you?" she demanded incredulously. "I've only met him once before, at our wedding."

"At which time, I remember, you enjoyed his company a great deal."

"I should think anyone would enjoy his company. He's fun."

"*Fun?*" Carlyle looked as if he'd never heard the word before. "Do you think this is about fun?"

"Yes," she said, giving him a warning look. "It's Christmas, and Christmas should be fun—for everyone. Especially Emma."

"Ah, yes, Emma. I'm glad you remembered her. Do you think she'd have understood your notion of fun?"

"What on earth—?"

"Suppose she'd seen you?"

"I honestly doubt if it would have bothered her. She's seen Denis kissing most people under the mistletoe today. That's what mistletoe is for."

He rounded on her, his face furious. "If you want to be kissed under the mistletoe, you have a perfectly good husband available for the purpose."

"Stop talking to me like an interdepartmental memo," she snapped back. "My 'perfectly good husband' has been oblivious to mistletoe all day."

"Well, we'll put that right now," he said, reaching for her swiftly.

The next moment she was pulled hard against him, her mouth crushed by his. There was anger in his movements, in the determined way he held her against him, his lips forcing hers to accept him. This was a new kind of passion, not the gentle loving kindness of the time they'd lain together, but a fierce, driving desperation that she could feel welling up in him, forcing him on.

Once before, on the night of the party, he'd kissed her like this, and she'd dreamed of it happening again. This was how she wanted him, not asking but demanding, taking insistently because possession was the only thing that mattered. The strong male body pressed close to hers was as unyielding as steel, and his arms held her in a grip that left her helpless.

"Carlyle . . ." she murmured.

"Shut up," he said against her mouth. "There's nothing to say."

No, there was nothing to say. There was nothing in the whole world but the mad pounding of the blood in her veins and the thrilling tremors that went through her at the insistence of his lips.

"I can't breathe," she gasped through the dizzying of her senses.

"Good," he grated. His lips trailed heatedly down her check to her throat. He was murmuring and she couldn't quite take in the words, but he might have said, "I've wanted you..."

"What—did you say?"

"Quiet. This is how you ought to be kissed. Do you know the difference *now* between a man and a boy?"

She could only gasp, "Yes—yes—"

"You're mine," he murmured. "You belong to me..."

"Yes..."

"The hell with bargains. You belong to *me*."

She was half out of her mind with pleasure and the unexpected happiness of this moment. If only it would go on forever.

"Carlyle—Carlyle—"

His face was above hers again, dark with some predatory emotion she'd never seen there before. "Let me hear you say 'Denis,'" he demanded.

"Denis—who?"

"That's better." His breath was still coming raggedly, but her answer seemed to have calmed him. There was tenderness in his lips again as he lowered them to hers. She was possessed by joy at the feel of his caressing mouth. This was how it ought always to be...

And then the spell was broken by one dreadful noise.

A smothered, childish giggle.

Like dreamers they pulled apart and turned horrified eyes to the kitchen doorway. It was empty but another giggle came from the hall. With a muttered sound Carlyle strode over and was just in time to see three children vanishing in different directions.

"Emma!"

A bland, innocent face appeared over the banisters. "Yes, Daddy?" she said meekly. "Did you want me?"

Carlyle sighed. "Not right at that moment, no," he said under his breath.

Briony was still rooted to the spot, shaking with the tumultuous thing that had happened to her, and the suddenness of its ending. Had he really said those things, or had her fevered brain imagined them? What would he say to her now?

He came back to her, looking rueful. "We should have remembered that we were practically in public. At least, I should. I'm sorry."

"No need to be sorry—"

"No, well—"

Paula appeared in the doorway. "Carlyle, you went to fetch some mince pies and were never heard of again. How like a man to go on a simple errand and forget what he went for!"

"Forget— Oh, yes, I forgot why I came in here. Briony, mince pies."

"They're here," she said, hoping her voice didn't shake.

"Come on, then," Paula urged. "Emma wants to play that word game where she beats us all hollow."

The house was silent. Downstairs, the tree still glowed. Upstairs, all was dark. Briony, coming out of her room to make a final check on Emma, found the little girl sitting on the stairs with Carlyle, whispering.

"Sorry, Daddy. Truly."

"You're not sorry at all. You were having the laugh of your life."

"Just a teeny, *little* laugh." Emma giggled. "It was nice to see you and Mummy like that."

"Well, I'm glad we gave you some fun," Carlyle said lightly.

"Not just fun. It was nice to think that you and Mummy—you know."

Briony saw him slip an arm round Emma's shoulders and draw her close. "As long as it made you happy," he said. "You are happy, aren't you?"

"Yes, Daddy."

"Really happy?"

"Really and truly."

"Then everything's all right. Because your happiness is the most important thing in the world."

"Thank you for a lovely Christmas."

"You should thank Mummy. Nobody knows how much she does for us."

"I do. I know."

"That's all right then. Come on. Time you were back in bed."

He lifted her in his arms. Briony stepped back into the shadows as Carlyle carried his child past. And neither of them saw her.

CHAPTER TEN

EVERYDAY that Emma lived was a gift. Better still, she showed no signs of failing. As February passed into March they began to hope that she would see the spring, perhaps even the summer. They watched her constantly, torturing themselves when she caught a tiny chill, rejoicing when she came through it. There were still alarms, times when she overexerted herself and collapsed, puffing. There were things she couldn't be allowed to do. But her strength held out better than they'd feared.

The ballet dress was still her favorite wear in the home. Emma had accidentally spilled grease on the first one and been so distraught that they immediately replaced it. It happened that Briony was confined to the house with a heavy cold, so rather than make Emma wait Carlyle went to the shop himself and collected the new one. Emma put it on at once, and Briony found her posing in front of the mirror, wearing not only the dress, but also a tiny swan's crown on her head.

"Isn't it lovely?" Emma asked. "Daddy gave it to me." She smiled. "I 'spec you picked it."

"No, I didn't, actually," Briony admitted. "I didn't even know he was going to get it."

"Truly?"

"Truly. He must have had the idea when he was in the shop."

A look of blissful content came over Emma's face. Briony understood its meaning. Emma loved her new

149

mother, but it was her father who held first place in her heart. And that was as it should be.

"You love Daddy very much, don't you?" she asked fondly.

Emma nodded. "Ever so and ever so," she confirmed. "He's the best Daddy in the world."

"Do you ever tell him so?"

Emma frowned, considering. "Well—not—just like that."

"I think you should. Just like that. It would mean so much to him."

Emma's little face grew suddenly very wise. "You love Daddy, too, don't you?"

"Yes," Briony said simply. With Carlyle she kept her secret, but with this child only the truth would do.

"Ever so?" Emma persisted anxiously.

"Ever so and ever so," Briony whispered.

Emma relaxed visibly, as though inwardly she were saying, "That's all right, then." Again Briony wondered just how much the little girl knew. Could she really be looking ahead, past the end of her own life, to the father who would be devastated without her? Surely it wasn't possible? Yet Emma's eyes were on her, gentle and full of an understanding that was too much for a child.

The following day, when they arrived at Brownies, Emma scampered straight off to join her friends. The Brown Owl signaled to Briony that she wanted a word, but was immediately distracted by a small Brownie with a question. By the time she'd sorted it out, the meeting was under way, and Briony was left wondering what Brown Owl wanted to talk about.

She soon found out. When it was time to leave Emma dashed across to Briony, big with news. "We're going away to camp," she said. "For a whole week."

Briony raised dismayed eyes to the Brown Owl who came hurrying toward her. "Go and get your things, darling," she told Emma.

When the child had gone, Briony said helplessly, "I can't possibly let her go to camp."

"I'm sorry," said the Brown Owl. "I meant to warn you so that you could tell her in advance that she couldn't go, but as you saw, I got sidetracked."

"Now she's got her hopes up and I've got a real problem," Briony said with a sigh.

All the way home Emma babbled merrily about the Brownie camp. Not until they were safely home did Briony say, "Darling, you must be realistic. You know you're not strong enough to go to camp."

"But everyone's going," Emma protested.

"Everyone else hasn't got a weak heart. I'm sorry to disappoint you, but it's impossible."

"But I *want* to," Emma wailed.

"I know," Briony said tenderly. "But we'll find some other treat for you."

"I don't *want* another treat. I want to go to camp."

"You're not strong enough—"

"I am, I am," Emma protested. "I'm heaps stronger now. Heaps and heaps—"

Briony dropped to one knee and tried to take Emma in her arms, but the child pushed her away.

"We'll go to the ballet that week," Briony pleaded.

"I don't want to go to the ballet." Emma wept. "I *hate* the ballet. And I hate you. I hate everyone." Her tears became noisy sobs.

From there it escalated into a full-scale tantrum. Briony's heart was wrung with pity for the child, denied her chance to enjoy life with other children, but she knew she must calm her down before she exhausted herself.

At last Emma solved the problem for her by running upstairs to her room and hurling herself on the bed in a passion of sobs. With any luck, Briony thought, she would cry herself to sleep. Sure enough, silence followed in a few minutes, and when she looked in to check, Emma was sleeping peacefully, clutching Oswald Penguin. Oswald Whale had been hurled onto the floor where he lay stranded, a forlorn testimony to Briony's fall from favor.

She called Carlyle to tell him what had happened.

"Is she all right?" he asked sharply.

"Yes, she's asleep. But when you come home she's going to start work on you, so I thought I'd warn you."

"There's no way I'll give in. I just think it's a pity this situation arose." He hung up, leaving Briony with the shocked realization that he blamed her.

But perhaps she really was to blame, she thought unhappily. If she hadn't insisted on letting Emma be a Brownie this would never have happened.

As she'd feared, Emma woke as soon as her father's car turned into the drive, and she came hurrying downstairs.

"Mummy says I can't go to Brownie camp, but I can, can't I, Daddy?"

"No, darling," he said gently but firmly. "You're not strong enough."

Emma stuck out her lower lip mutinously. "It's not *fair*."

"No, it's not fair," Carlyle agreed. "It's not fair that you're ill when other little girls are well."

"But I'm not ill," Emma shouted. "I'm better now and I want to go to camp."

Carlyle shook his head. Recognizing final authority, Emma gave up the argument and kicked the furniture instead.

"That's enough, Emma," Briony said.

For answer Emma kicked the furniture again.

"Go up to your room," Briony said firmly. "I won't have that kind of behavior."

Emma met her eyes, as if calculating whether to risk another kick, then seemed to think better of it. Turning, she began to trail disconsolately upstairs.

"Look," Carlyle said in a low voice, "does she really need to—"

"Yes," Briony said. "Just for a while. She can come down later."

Carlyle went into the front room and poured himself a drink. "Why the hell did this have to happen?"

"You blame me, don't you?"

"Are you surprised? I said she shouldn't join the Brownies."

"She's loved it there."

"Until now. This was bound to happen."

"Would it have been better to keep her under lock and key? Surely it was better for her to have some pleasure in her last few— Oh, my God!"

Her horrified eyes were fixed on something over Carlyle's shoulder. He turned to see the trouble and for a moment they both stood petrified at the sight of Emma climbing down a tree immediately outside the house. As they watched she missed her footing and slithered down several feet, finally saving herself by grabbing at branches.

It was only a short distance through the hall and out of the front door, but it seemed to take them an eternity while visions of the worst that might happen to Emma shuddered through Briony's brain. They arrived as she was scrambling down the last few feet. She reached the ground, gasping and holding on to the tree. Without hesitation Carlyle scooped her up into his arms.

"Call the doctor," he told Briony through gritted teeth. "Get him over here at once."

"I'm all right, Daddy," Emma protested through gasps. But he was already running toward the house with her.

Briony called the doctor, then hurried upstairs to Emma's room. She was lying on the bed and seemed cross at the fuss that was being made about her.

"I'm all *right*, Daddy," she said insistently.

"We'll let the doctor decide that," Carlyle said, very pale. He looked up sharply at Briony. "Is he coming?"

"He'll be here in a few minutes." To Briony's relief Emma's color was good and her breathing was easier. But Carlyle seemed not to have noticed these hopeful signs. He was regarding his daughter with a look of terror and anguish.

Dr. Canning arrived and talked to Emma like an old friend. Then he asked to be left alone with her. As they waited for him downstairs, Carlyle said, "I'm sorry for what I said. It was cruel and stupid."

"Then you don't blame me?"

"No, I just lashed out because I was frightened, but you're the best friend I have. Without you—"

At that moment the doctor came in. His first words fell on them like a blow. "I should like to take Emma into hospital tomorrow."

"Oh, God," Carlyle said, turning his head away.

"No, no, it's not what you think," the old man told him. "The fact is that she seems stronger than I'd expected. She took that fall remarkably well. I'd like to do some tests.''

As Carlyle seemed too dazed to speak, Briony said, ''Do you mean— You can't mean that Emma's actually getting better?''

''Let's say that she's improved a little. She can't really recover without that operation, but if she's fighting back as well as I think she is—well, it may be something to consider again.''

Carlyle stared. ''Are you saying that she actually has a chance of life?''

''Let's do the tests, and then we'll see,'' the doctor said cautiously.

Carlyle suddenly seemed like a man in a state of shock. It was Briony who asked, ''Have you told any of this to Emma?''

Dr. Canning's eyes twinkled. ''It was more of a case of her telling me. She kept insisting that she was better. At first I dismissed it as wishful thinking, but then I thought perhaps I should listen to her. She jumped at the idea of tests. She's sure they'll prove her right.''

''But—how has this happened?'' Carlyle asked in a dazed voice. ''We were all so sure that she was slipping away.''

''She was, once. And without an operation she'll lose what she's gained. But she has great determination. And perhaps—'' The doctor's wise eyes rested on Briony. ''Perhaps there are also other reasons, things that medical science can't put in a bottle.''

Briony showed him to the door. She returned to find Carlyle rooted to the same spot. ''Did you hear what he said?'' he asked.

''Every word,'' Briony confirmed. She was dazed with hope.

"But it couldn't be true, could it? *Could it?*"

Their eyes met. The next moment they'd thrown themselves into each other's arms, hugging fiercely. "It can be true," Briony cried. "We've got to believe that. *She* believes it. We can't let her down."

He drew back to look at her. "And it's all due to you. That's what he was saying. You made her strong again."

"We both did."

"Let's go up and see her."

Like two excited children they raced up the stairs to find the object of their concern regarding them with an air of triumph.

Emma went into hospital next day. Briony went, too, settling into a small room with a connecting door. As the doctor had said, Emma was full of enthusiasm, and it carried her through the tedious round of tests and the endless questions.

At the end of the third day Dr. Canning said, "She's definitely stronger. We now have a window of opportunity. I told you she had about eight months. That was nearly five months ago. Now I'm going to say eight months again, starting from now."

"And that's the best she can hope for?" Carlyle demanded.

"Yes, unless—"

"Unless?" Briony asked in agony.

"I once gave Emma only a ten percent chance of surviving an operation. Now I'd put it as high as fifty-fifty."

Carlyle gripped Briony's hand painfully. "But if we waited, surely her chances would improve again?" he persisted.

The doctor shook his head. "No, she's reached a peak. From here she'll slip back."

The grip on Briony's hand grew tighter. "If she has this operation—and it fails—she'd still have some time left, wouldn't she?"

The doctor's eyes were full of pity as he shook his head. "If it fails," he said gently, "she won't come round."

Carlyle was beginning to gasp as if he were fighting for breath. "But surely we don't have to make a decision right this minute? A few days—"

"Not even that. The best surgeon in this field is David Warfield. He usually works abroad, but by a lucky chance he happens to be in this country for a week. I've already spoken to him, and he could do it tomorrow."

"Tomorrow!" Carlyle exclaimed. "No, it's too soon. I need time to think."

"I'm afraid I can only give you an hour before I have to let the surgeon know." Dr. Canning added gently, "I know that fifty-fifty still isn't very good odds."

"I need to get out of here," Carlyle said harshly.

Briony followed him as far as the car park, but before he reached the car he stopped. "I must walk," he said. "I just can't take all this in."

Although it was only early evening, darkness had fallen, and the streets gleamed with the rain that had fallen earlier. Briony fell into step beside him and they walked in silence for a mile, Carlyle setting such a pace that she had to hurry to keep up.

After a while they reached a park. Carlyle made his way across the grass to a children's playground, with roundabouts and swings. In summer it must have been an enchanting place, but now it was bleak and deserted. He went to sit on one of the low benches, and Briony sat beside him.

"I used to bring Emma here, a couple of years ago," he said. "She'd shin right up to the top of the climbing frame, and hang from her knees while I stood below, terrified." He gave a short laugh. "She wasn't bothered."

He pointed to the three slides, one small, one medium and big. "You're supposed to start on the little one and work your way up to the big one," he said.

"But I expect she went straight onto the big one," Briony said.

"Yes. And the seesaw. She loved that, until she began to find it tame. She liked being 'bumped.' Do you know what that means?"

"Going up and down very hard and fast, so that you hit the ground with a bump," Briony said. "I used to do it. The harder, the better."

"She came down terribly hard once, and caught her foot underneath. I thought that would cure her, but next time she just did it again. She had so much energy and courage. She was so strong—" His voice shook.

Briony put her arms about him. There was nothing even she could say to help him at this moment.

"I can't do it," he said harshly. "I can't let them take her into an operating theater tomorrow, knowing that I may never see her again. *I can't do it.*"

"Not even to give her a chance of life?" Briony whispered.

"Life?" he demanded bitterly. "Does she really have a chance of life? You heard him. Fifty-fifty. What kind of odds are those?"

"They're better odds than she'll have in eight months' time," Briony reminded him. "I know it looks hard now, but suppose you say no. How will you feel when the time comes for her to die? You'll wish then that you'd seized the chance. It'll be too late, and you'll regret it for the rest of your life."

He turned a livid face onto her. "You want me to do this?" he demanded. "Do you know what you're asking?"

"Of course I know," she reminded him.

"She's stronger than she's been in months—but she could be gone in a few hours—"

"I know," she cried in agony. "I've been through that. I've lived for months with two images in my mind— Sally full of life and energy, and Sally dead and cold— and only a few hours between them. That's what's so terrible—how it can change so quickly."

"And knowing that, you still want me to take the risk?"

"Is anything too much to ask, for her?"

Dumbly he shook his head. "But I don't know if I can make myself do it," he said. "I've never thought of myself as a coward, but I am—unless you're there—"

She took his hand and held it tight against her breast, enfolded in both hers, wondering if he was ready for what she had to say next.

"There someone else I think we should ask," she said.

"Who?"

"Emma herself. It's her life. Tell her the odds, and if she wants to take the risk, that's it. I think I know what her answer will be."

He looked at her a long time without speaking. The hand she held was dreadfully cold. At last he nodded. Together they left the park and returned to the hospital.

Emma was sitting propped up by pillows. She looked alert and happy, and her color was good. Briony's heart almost failed her. Within a few hours...

When they'd all hugged each other, she looked at Carlyle, waiting for him to speak. But his eyes, meeting hers, were desperate, and he held on to his daughter's hand as though he would never let it go.

"The doctor thinks I'm better," Emma declared with the light of battle in her eyes. "He's amazed at how strong I am."

"Yes, you are stronger," Briony said, sitting on the bed. "But you'll never be really strong until they do something about that wonky heart of yours. It won't get well on its own."

Briony hesitated, uncertain how to say the next bit. But then her eyes met Emma's. The child's exuberance had been replaced by a kind of gravity, as though Emma had suddenly understood that the time for childish things was past. Carlyle said nothing, but sat looking from one to the other, understanding that they were communicating without words.

"Can they do it now?" Emma asked at last.

"It depends on you," Briony said. "If you want to."

"What is this?" Carlyle asked. He looked at Emma. "Am I imagining things? How much do you—"

"I was sure Emma knew," Briony said.

There was something almost motherly in the way the child patted his hand. "You didn't want me to know, so I didn't. But I always knew really."

"But—how?"

"You always had time to take me out," she said simply.

There was nothing for Carlyle to say, nothing for him to do but bow his head. Emma reached up her arms to him to enfold him in a gesture that was oddly mature in its protectiveness. Briony watched them for a moment before leaving the room. It was up to them now. Her part was done.

She waited in the corridor for about half an hour, until the doctor came to find her. "I'm afraid I have to know soon," he said.

At that moment the door opened and Carlyle emerged. He looked at the other two for a moment, then nodded without speaking.

"I'll call David Warfield at once," said the doctor, and hurried away.

Carlyle sat beside Briony. He seemed very calm. "She's not afraid," he said. "All this time I've thought I was protecting her, but she—" His voice shook and he buried his head in his hands. He recovered himself at once. "She knows what she wants. All or nothing. You were right. She never even thought of compromising." He was silent for a moment, then he spoke again in a strained voice. "She knew she might be dying because I made time for her."

"Don't brood about it," Briony said. "It isn't as important as the things that draw you together."

He nodded. "She spoke about Helen," he said. "If the end comes—she'll be with her. That's why she's not afraid."

Dr. Canning came bustling back. "It's all set. The surgeon will be here early tomorrow." His face softened as he looked at them. "He's the best there is."

Carlyle nodded. "Can we stay with her tonight?"

"Of course. But try not to let her talk. The nurse will be giving her a mild sedative so that she gets a good night's sleep." He saw a slight change come over Carlyle's face. "Is something the matter?"

"I—no," Carlyle said hurriedly.

But Briony understood. Tonight of all nights Carlyle might have been able to do what had always been so difficult, to open his heart to his child, and speak freely. It could have been his last chance. But it was too late. Emma's journey had begun. The tide was rushing on, carrying her with it, perhaps forever.

CHAPTER ELEVEN

EMMA looked up excitedly as they went into her room, and Carlyle smiled at her. It was the hardest thing he'd ever done. "All ready for the big day?"

She nodded vigorously. "I wish it was tomorrow," she said.

"Do—do you, darling?" he just managed to say.

"I want them to do the operation, and then it'll be over and I'll be better. And I'll go to camp and do ballet classes and—and everything." She looked anxiously at Briony. "I can, can't I, Mummy?"

"You can do anything you want, darling."

She sighed. "That's all right, then."

Carlyle met Briony's eyes and she knew what he was thinking. How could he say the things he wanted to say, things that would imply goodbye, to this child who was so confident of recovery?

While he wrestled with his dilemma the door opened and a nurse came in. "It's time for her sedative," she said.

Emma swallowed the pill and lay back. Her eyes were still open but already she was growing drowsy. " 'Night, Mummy," she murmured. " 'Night, Daddy."

They kissed her, then sat, one each side of her bed, watching until she fell asleep. She lay almost motionless for the whole night, while they kept vigil over her, knowing that it might be for the last time.

She woke early. "Is it tomorrow yet?" was her first question.

"Yes," Briony assured her.

Carlyle took Emma's hand and looked into her face. It seemed to Briony that words trembled on his lips, the words he'd never known how to say before, but could surely say now.

And then, suddenly, it was too late. A nurse bustled in, then another. In moments the machine was in motion. Despite the early hour David Warfield was there already, greeting Emma cheerfully. In appearance he was the most nondescript man Briony had ever seen, of medium height and coloring and indeterminate age. Even his voice was without personality. But Dr. Canning had insisted that for this operation there was no one like him in the world.

He had a few kindly words for Emma's parents, but quickly returned his attention to his patient. "The sooner we get started, the better," he said.

As Emma was about to be wheeled away, she said, "Goodbye, Mummy. Goodbye, Daddy."

"Goodbye, darling," they both said.

Then she was gone, spirited away to regions where they couldn't follow her.

"Goodbye," Carlyle murmured.

"She didn't mean it like that," Briony said.

"I know. She's so brave—and so small."

Hours passed. They sat holding hands, speaking now and then. But there was really nothing to say. Once the door at the end of the corridor opened and a nurse came hurrying through. They tensed, sure that she'd come to tell them the worst, but she passed by and out of sight. They fell back, feeling their hearts thudding painfully.

Another hour. Two. The nurse who'd given Emma the sedative approached, walking at a sedate pace. She stopped in front of them.

"I'm sorry—" she said in a tone of gentle concern.

It was all over. The nightmare had happened. Emma was dead. Carlyle's hand froze to Briony's and his face was ghastly.

The nurse was still speaking. "Sorry you've had to wait all this time. It's taking a little longer than we thought."

The world returned to some sort of normality. Briony whispered, "What?"

"It took a little longer than Dr. Warfield expected. He's finishing now."

"You mean, she's alive?"

"Yes, she's holding on. They'll be wheeling her into Intensive Care soon. You can go along there and I'll bring you some tea."

At the door of Intensive Care they met David Warfield who told them that the next twenty-four hours would be critical. They could sit with her.

Worst of all was seeing Emma lying, a small, frail figure, amid a mountain of machinery. She was attached to tubes, monitors, drips, and she lay frighteningly still. A nurse watched her closely. There was only room for one other person beside Emma's bed.

"You sit with her," Briony whispered. "I'll call Joyce and tell her how it went."

Hour after hour. The thin green line went across the monitor screen, its regular blips reassuring them of life. Every breath was a victory. Carlyle sat still until his body ached. At last he rose and went to join Briony, sitting a little distance off. They stayed together in silence, until suddenly he said, "You were right."

"About what?"

"You said I should talk to her. I wish now that I had. I didn't know how, but I should have tried. I told myself I'd done everything for her. I gave her you, the best gift of all. But I know that I was really trying to cover my own deficiencies. And now—now—I think of all the things I'd like to say to her—and perhaps I'll never get the chance."

"But you do have the chance," Briony said urgently. "You have it now."

"But she couldn't hear me."

"You don't know that. Unconscious people can often hear things. The doctors told me that at the hospital when Sally was ill. And I know it's true."

He looked at her quickly. "How?"

"Because—" It was the most painful secret of all, and one she'd thought she could never speak of, but she would risk any pain for this man. "Because when Sally was in a coma, in her last moments I took her hand and told her that I loved her. And I felt her squeeze. She hadn't moved until then, but she squeezed my hand quite firmly. That was the last thing she did. It was her way of saying that she'd heard me, that she understood. It was her goodbye, too, but at least I know that she died knowing how much I loved her."

He looked across at Emma. "Couldn't you—"

"No," Briony said. It hurt her to refuse him anything at such a moment, but she couldn't afford to weaken about this, for Emma's sake, and for Carlyle's in the long years ahead.

"It's you she needs," she said. "Because if the worst happens, and you have to give her up—" He bent his head in agony, and she stroked it tenderly. "If that happens," she whispered, "you won't be giving her up into a void. Helen will be there to receive her from you. And it must be you who does that, not me. It must be your hands that give her to Helen. Do you see?"

After a long moment Carlyle raised his head. His face was deadly pale but very calm. He went to sit beside Emma and took her hand in his. Leaning forward, he began to talk to her quietly.

At first Briony couldn't hear what he said, but as night fell and the ward grew quieter she caught some of the murmured words, and knew he was talking about the funfair. She heard, "Oswald and Oswald," then her own name.

It was hard for him, talking to someone who never responded, and after a while his inspiration dried up and he looked to her in urgent plea.

"Talk about the wedding," she suggested.

He gave her a look of gratitude, and began telling Emma how lovely she'd looked coming down the aisle, the horse-drawn carriage, anything he could remember.

Night. A new shift of nurses arrived and Carlyle had to leave the bed while they performed their routines, checking, making notes. There was tea, sandwiches, the offer of beds for the night. But they declined. They wouldn't leave her.

"Talk about the future," Briony advised him. "About the things you're going to do together."

He nodded and took Emma's hand back into his.

"You'll be well again soon," he told her, "and you can start dancing class again. Mummy would have been a ballerina if she hadn't married me. When you were born she said you'd be a better dancer than she could have been. And you will be. I'll come to see you dance, and I'll be so proud."

Briony moved away, dismayed at a little feeling of hurt that tugged at her heart. She couldn't be thinking of herself now. But the way Carlyle had said "Mummy," obviously meaning Helen, had given her a small shock.

For months Emma and Carlyle himself had called her Mummy. But Emma's real mother was Helen, and as the little girl lay between life and death it was Helen who was with her. And it was right that it should be so.

She went out into the corridor. The other two didn't need her now. She drank some more tea, and called Joyce again to say that Emma was holding on. But everything she did had a dreamlike quality.

When she returned to the ward Carlyle was still talking softly to Emma, the inspiration now seeming to come without trouble. Briony sat by the wall and watched them. Now and then she heard the word "Mummy," She tried not to listen but she couldn't help it. As the small hours wore away she knew that the flash of physical jealousy she'd felt for Deirdre was nothing to the jealousy of the heart she felt for Helen.

Emma had lain all night without moving. It seemed impossible that her spirit could fight on longer against weariness and pain. As the dawn broke Carlyle looked down at his child and it seemed to him that she was smaller, as though she was already slipping away. He took her hand and placed his lips close to her ear. There was one thing still to be said, something that all the talking came down to in the end.

"I love you, my darling," he whispered. "I'll always love you."

And it was there, unmistakable, the slight squeezing on his hand from a little girl at the last of her strength. He looked up at Briony, who'd come to the bed. "She heard me."

"Yes. She knows that you love her."

"She squeezed my hand. Like Sally. You said—"

"Look," Briony said through her tears. "Look."

Slowly Emma's eyes were opening. They were fixed on her father's face. "Hello, Daddy," she said.

He stroked her face. "I thought you'd gone away from me."

"But you were there with me."

"Was I?"

"All the time. Mummy was there, too. She said it would be all right." She smiled and closed her eyes again.

Then the medical machine took over. Nurses came, and doctors, checking, monitors, smiles of relief and happiness. Briony went to the window and stood looking out. The light was growing stronger all the time, a brilliant daybreak full of hope and promise. And suddenly she had to close her eyes, because the light hurt them.

Emma recovered fast. With her heart functioning efficiently at last, strength flowed back into her limbs, color returned to her cheeks and her breathlessness vanished.

After a few days in Intensive Care she was put into a little sunny room on the ground floor, overlooking the gardens. Outside the spring daffodils made a riot of yellow. Everywhere new life was bursting, underlining the dramatic change that had come into their lives without warning.

Every evening Carlyle hurried to the hospital from work. Emma would fling her arms open wide to him, and be gathered into a bear hug. Briony would watch them fondly, smiling. They'd found each other in a way that hadn't been true before.

Emma's attitude to herself was unchanged. She accepted Briony as her mother as unquestioningly as before. Which was strange, Briony thought, after what had happened to Emma as she lay between life and death.

The two people with her then had been Carlyle and Helen. Briony had come nowhere. Yet Emma almost seemed to have forgotten the experience, and Briony couldn't bring herself to question the child.

She was happy for Emma and Carlyle, yet there was a faint, half-acknowledged ache in her heart that wouldn't go away. She felt stranded in limbo. In the language of the business world, where Carlyle was king, the terms under which she'd married him were no longer valid. The conditions were null and void. The contract rested on a false premise.

It would have been easy just to let things drift. For Emma's sake, Carlyle would never ask her to leave. They could have a contented life, growing closer over the years, having their own children, until perhaps at last the origins of their marriage became blurred with time. The voice of the tempter whispered that it would be better than life without him.

But would it? Some deep, uncompromising part of Briony's nature, something that wouldn't settle for second best, refused to let it go at that. She could say nothing until Emma had completely regained her health. But the time was coming when she and Carlyle must face the truth, whatever that might lead to.

One evening Carlyle arrived for his visit to find Briony just leaving Emma's room. "I've got to see the doctor about the arrangements for taking her home," she said. "Any day now."

"Great. Can't be too soon for me." Briony vanished down the corridor. Carlyle went in and enfolded Emma in a bear hug. For a while they made gleeful plans for her return, but he soon became aware that she was distracted. "What's the matter, darling?"

"Daddy, I've lost Oswald. He fell off the bed."

Carlyle ducked but could see nothing. "Are you sure?"

"I'm sure I've lost him. If he's not there he must be somewhere else."

"You stay in bed. I'll find him. Which one am I looking for?"

"Oswald."

"Yes, but which Oswald?"

"*Oswald.*"

At last Carlyle located the whale and the penguin lying together on the floor. Emma opened her arms for them and thanked him.

"You had me pretty confused there, for a while," he told her. "I didn't know if I was looking for one or two."

"But they're both Oswald. Oswald and Oswald *is* Oswald. Don't you see?"

"I'm beginning to, darling." Carlyle got up from the floor and dusted himself down, muttering something.

"What was that, Daddy?"

"Nothing," he said hastily.

"It sounded like 'saucepan.' "

Emma returned home to great rejoicing. There were cards and gifts from all the family, and a letter from Denis full of drawings of matchstick men that made her giggle. The milestones began to slip by, her first day back at school, her first evening with the Brownies, her first dancing class.

One night, when Emma was in bed, Briony said casually, "Have you given any thought to what happens now?"

He frowned. "Why should anything happen now?"

She took a deep breath and spoke brightly. "Really, Carlyle, you're very forgetful. You hired me for six months, and the six months are up. They've ended more happily than we hoped, and that's fine. But it really is time for me to get on with my own life now."

There was a short silence before he replied. "I didn't know you felt like that—"

"It was only a temporary bargain," she reminded him.

"But you and Emma have grown so close. I thought— aren't you happy with us?"

"I'm delighted it's worked out so well for you both," Briony said, choosing her words carefully. "But after all, a promise is a promise, and you always said you were a man of your word. Neither of us anticipated this situation."

He stared at her, and she saw the anger gather in his face. "And that's all it is to you?" he snapped. "A situation? Are you really prepared to simply walk out on Emma, when you mean so much to her?"

Say how much I mean to you, she thought. *Please say that.*

After a moment she replied, "I'm not going to walk out. I wouldn't do that to her. But there's a business course I'd like to enrol in. It's about sixty miles away from here, so I'll have to find digs. We don't have to make any dramatic announcements to Emma. I'll just fade out of the picture gradually. With all the new things in her life, she'll hardly notice."

"Do you really think that?" he asked coldly. "Or is it just a convenient excuse to do what you want?"

Ask me to stay because you want me. Tell me that all we've been through together means something.

"For heaven's sake, Carlyle, look at Emma's life. She's doing well at school now she's going full time. She's got lots of friends. She'll be going to stay with Elaine and her children, then she's got Brownie camp. And the next thing will be ballet school. I've really played such a small part in her life that she'll hardly notice me gone, if we go about it the right way."

"And what, in your view, is the right way?" he demanded in a colder voice than she'd ever heard him use.

"Joyce called me today. Your father is going on a painting holiday next month. He'll be away for six weeks. I thought Joyce could come here."

"To cover your exit, you mean?" Carlyle demanded ironically.

"To be here for Emma so that she doesn't feel any lack. You know they adore each other."

He regarded her, his head on one side. "You get on well with my mother, don't you?"

"Yes. I think she's lovely."

"She loves you, too. So do all my family. Not just Emma, but all of them. Even my sister Paula, who takes offence at everybody on principle, talks kindly about you. But that's not enough for you, is it?"

"No," she said with a little sigh. "It's not enough for me."

"Well, I suppose you'll do what you want to do," he growled. "And never mind how anybody else feels about it."

Tell me how you feel about it. Not the rest of the family. You.

"I shall need your help, Carlyle. The college only takes students 'of proven ability.' A letter from you should smooth my path."

"A letter recommending my own wife? How much attention will they pay to that?"

"You're right. I'd better use my maiden name."

He scowled. "I should have expected that, I suppose. All right, I'll give you the letter. And be damned to you."

CHAPTER TWELVE

WITH Carlyle's recommendation Briony had no trouble being accepted into the college. She began to spend weekdays in digs, returning home at the weekends. Joyce regarded the arrangement with raised eyebrows, but held her tongue, and Emma, too, said surprisingly little. She was happy with her life filled with new interests, and at weekends she greeted Briony cheerfully.

Usually Briony drove back on Sunday night, but one weekend she stayed over until Monday morning, and was still there when Carlyle left for work. He returned that evening to find Joyce and Emma playing draughts.

"Did Briony get off all right this morning?" he asked gruffly, throwing himself into a chair with relief.

"I dropped her at the station," Joyce informed him.

There was a silence, during which Carlyle became aware that his daughter and his mother were exchanging glances. "What?" he asked.

"We think it's time you told us what's going on," Joyce said.

"Why should anything be going on?" he demanded.

"Because Mummy said she wouldn't be coming back next weekend," Emma said.

"She's very busy with this course," Carlyle said lamely.

"Is that all?" Joyce asked.

He threw her a look that meant "not in front of Emma," but she seemed not to see it.

"You're making a mountain out of a molehill, both of you," he said.

"Why is Mummy so dreadfully unhappy?" Emma demanded.

"Honestly, darling, you imagined that—"

"No, I didn't. She *is* unhappy." Emma fixed her father with an accusing look. "You didn't know, did you?"

"I—no, I didn't."

"You should have known," Joyce informed him.

"How could I?" He looked to Emma for support, but found her regarding him accusingly. "I gather you both think it's my fault."

"It probably is," Joyce observed.

"I didn't want her to go," he said, goaded. "There was no need. I told her she was being ridiculous."

Emma and Joyce spoke with one outraged voice. "You said *that*?"

"There are things—Briony and I—" He looked helplessly at Emma. "Things were different when you were ill. You nearly died. You needed her then."

It might have been his fancy that his daughter regarded him with pity. "But what about you?" she asked. "Don't you need Mummy?"

He stared. After a moment he recovered himself. "Darling, there's a lot you don't understand—"

"Don't treat the child like a fool," Joyce said bracingly. "It seems to me that *Emma's* not the one who doesn't understand."

In the silence that followed this pronouncement Carlyle seemed to hear the air singing around his ears. He had a feeling that the earth had shifted on its axis, leaving everything the same but totally transformed.

"I think the sooner you get Briony back, the better," Joyce went on, as if nothing had happened. "Then perhaps you'll stop acting like a bear with a sore head."

He was about to defend himself, when he caught Emma's eyes on him again and something warned him to watch what he said. "Is that what I've been doing?" he asked her meekly.

She nodded. "Horrible," she confirmed. "Especially if the phone rings, and it isn't her."

"Look, darling, it's better to face facts. The real reason Briony went away is—" It was strange how hard he found it to say the words. "I guess—she just doesn't love me. She loves you—but not me."

Emma frowned. "But she does love you."

"No, she doesn't."

"She *does*."

"She doesn't."

"Does!"

Carlyle almost said "Doesn't!" but checked himself in time, wondering where his wits had wandered. Father and daughter squared up to each other, while Joyce muttered, "Heaven give me patience!"

"Honestly, Daddy!" Emma said, regarding him with exasperated sympathy.

Carlyle looked from Emma to Joyce and back again. He'd always known that his daughter was a mixture of Helen and himself. Now it occurred to him that she was uncomfortably like his mother, as well.

"You've got it all wrong," he said. "Briony doesn't love me."

"She told me she did," Emma announced.

"That's imposs—when?"

"Weeks ago. I asked her and she said she loved you ever so and ever so," Emma finished with a triumphant air.

At the sound of the childish phrase a kind of tense eagerness went out of Carlyle. He gave a forced smile. "Of course she did, darling. I expect you had a lovely talk."

Sensing disbelief, Emma eyed him indignantly. "She said ever so and ever so," she insisted. "Nobody says ever so and ever so, unless it's true."

"So now you know," Joyce observed.

Carlyle rose, scowling. "I think the two of you have taken leave of your senses," he growled. "This is reality, not a fairy tale, and the reality is that Briony was here for Emma's sake, not mine. You were ill, darling, but you're not ill now, and Briony wants to get back to her own life."

"Well, that's your fault," Joyce said.

"Codswallop!" Carlyle said angrily, making for the door.

Emma seized her notepad. "Cods—"

"Two l's," Carlyle snapped, and walked out.

When she'd first started attending the college Briony had worried in case she wasn't up to the work. But she soon found that her powerful memory and tidy mind handled everything easily, and she grew in confidence. This, she decided, was what nature had intended her to be. Her love for Carlyle was no more than an aberration, best put behind her and forgotten. She told herself this very firmly, very often.

By day, with plenty to occupy her mind, she managed fairly well. But at night, lying alone in the darkness, her body would ache with longing for Carlyle's arms around her. But the real ache was in her heart.

She constantly tormented herself, wondering if she'd done the right thing. Shouldn't she have stayed with Carlyle for Emma's sake? But Emma didn't really need her anymore, not the way she'd once done.

As for Carlyle himself, of course he'd wanted her to stay with Emma. But Briony knew that if she'd accepted those terms she would have felt like a pensioner, kept on the strength out of kindness. It was better this way. The future stretched out before her, in which she would become successful and probably rich, using her mind in the way it was meant to be used. And using her heart not at all.

Carlyle blinked at the computer screen where the figures were beginning to dance. It was three in the morning and he should have been asleep long ago, but he was oddly reluctant to go upstairs these days. The king-size bed, which had so exactly suited him in the past, now felt like a desert.

He left the computer and went to sprawl on the sofa. Through the sleep that began to overtake him he thought he heard his study door open and close. He blinked again, wondering if he was imagining the small, dressing-gowned figure who stood there. But then the figure gave him a very tangible prod, and said, "Daddy!"

He rubbed his eyes. "What are you doing up at this hour?"

"I wanted to talk to you."

"Can't it wait until morning?"

"No. It's about Mummy."

He pulled himself together. "Darling, we said it all this afternoon."

"No," Emma said earnestly. "I mean Mummy—*and* Mummy."

He stared at her and spoke cautiously. "I'm not sure that I—" Something warned him that what he said next would be important. After a moment enlightenment came to him. "Do you mean, like Oswald and Oswald?"

She gave a sigh of relief. "I knew you'd understand."

"Not everything. Perhaps you'd better explain."

He held out an arm, crooked in invitation. Emma snuggled up on the sofa beside him, and began to tell him all about it.

The sound of a knock on her door at nine in the evening sent Briony across the floor with a fast-beating heart.

"Oh, it's you," she said, unable to keep the disappointment out of her voice.

Denis sighed. "Well, that tells me what I wanted to know. Don't I even get offered a cup of coffee?"

Briony pulled herself together. "Come in, Denis. It's nice to see you."

"But it would have been far nicer to see Carlyle, eh? Now what does that shrug mean?"

"It means that things are over between Carlyle and me. I don't even think of him these days."

"Little liar. You hated me for not being him."

Briony gave a wan smile. "Only for a moment. What are you doing in this neck of the woods?"

"I came to see you, of course. I thought there might be a chance for me now, but you've already answered that."

"Sit down and tell me all the news. How is—everybody?"

"I can't tell you much. Carlyle never exactly sought my company, and since he knew I was attracted to you I'm persona non grata."

"That's nonsense. Carlyle and I married for Emma's sake. He never cared for me."

"Now who's talking nonsense? He was jealous as hell when he caught me giving you that little peck at Christmas."

"He wasn't jealous. He was only afraid that Emma would see."

Denis was silent for a moment before saying, "Briony, for a clever woman, you're an awful fool. But then, your husband's an even bigger one. Ah, coffee! Thank you!"

He stayed for half an hour, talking his usual nonsense, but then, with more sensitivity than she would have given him credit for, he left her in peace. Briony was left to ponder his words. They seemed to contain some hope, but she'd finished with hope. Whatever might have been between herself and Carlyle was over, and that was that.

When the second knock came, she was already in bed. She pulled on a dressing gown to make her way sleepily across the floor. She thought it was Denis again, and as she opened the door she was already saying, "You can't come here at this time of—" Then she stopped, staring, while her breath came quickly.

"Can I come in?" Carlyle asked. She stood back in silence and closed the door behind him. They regarded each other. "Who did you think I was?" he asked. "Denis?"

She found her voice. "He called on me earlier."

"I know. I saw him arrive and I waited to see how long he stayed."

"Barely half an hour," she whispered. There was something in Carlyle's face that she'd never seen there before, and it made her heart suddenly beat madly.

"Yes, half an hour," he repeated. "And I tell you this. If he'd stayed all night, I'd have gone away and never seen you again."

"There was never any question of that. Why are you here, Carlyle?"

He looked at her a long moment in silence before saying, "I came to take you home."

"This is my home now."

"This will never be your home. Your home is with me, and Emma. If you want all this—" He indicated her books. "You can have it. You can do any job you want if it means that much to you."

"Carlyle, you don't know what means a lot to me and what doesn't."

He frowned. "That's what they said."

"They?"

"Emma and my mother."

"Are you here because they sent you?"

"Yes—no—it's something much more than that. It's hard to explain. The only thing I'm clear about is that I want you back. The house isn't a home without you." He saw that her face was still unyielding, and knew he still hadn't said the right thing. Alarm gripped him. He was The Great Fixer, whose silver tongue reduced rivals to furious silence. But only the right words would help him now, and he didn't know what they were.

"I don't understand," Briony said. "Denis left an hour ago. If you saw him, why did you wait so long before knocking?"

And suddenly he knew what the words were. "I was afraid," he said simply.

"You? Afraid?"

"It matters so much. If I get it wrong—and you don't love me—"

She couldn't be sure she'd heard him right. Incredulously she whispered, "Love you?"

"Emma says you do. She says you told her so. I thought she must have got it wrong, but she insisted that you'd said, 'ever so and ever so.' To her that means it must be true." He looked at her, an urgent question in his eyes.

"Oh, you fool," she breathed. "You complete fool."

"I know I'm a fool," he said with rare humility. "The only question is, what sort of a fool?"

She answered in the only way she could, putting her arms around him and laying her lips on his in the first kiss of their mutual love. For a moment he seemed too stunned to react. But then life returned to his limbs and he seized her in a fierce embrace.

"I love you," he said again and again. "I've loved you for months, but I couldn't find a way to tell you. You were so distant."

"I thought that was what you wanted. You kept reminding me that you were only doing it for Emma—that we had a bargain..."

"Don't you understand? *I love you.*" He stopped abruptly, for she had covered his mouth with her own. This was her kiss, her assertion of power, the moment when she claimed him.

"I was trying to reassure you," he said when he could breathe again. "I knew the bargain was important to you—"

"To hell with the bargain!" she said fiercely against his mouth. "Do you think I married you for money and a career in business? Is that what you really thought?"

"I don't know what I think anymore. Nothing that I believed seems to be true."

"This is true," she murmured, brushing her lips softly against his.

"Yes," he groaned. "This is true—only this—"

"My love, why are we wasting time?"

"You're right," he said, lifting her in his arms and kicking open the bedroom door. "We've years ahead for explanations. Let them wait. Briony—my darling—"

It was like making love for the first time. The past didn't count. All that mattered was now, discovering each other as lovers. The discovery was beautiful, warm with the sweetness of mutual giving and taking, and full of promise for their life together, now and forever.

Afterward, lying wrapped in each other's arms, they dozed in blissful content, then woke and discovered more bliss. "I can't believe that you really love me," she murmured.

"Believe it," he whispered, holding her body close to his.

"But how, when?

"It crept up on me. You were so beautiful coming down the aisle toward me. I'd only thought of you for Emma, but suddenly you were enchanting. But you'd been so reluctant to marry me—"

"Only because of Sally."

"I didn't know that. I thought I should tread carefully. Sometimes you seemed to be warming toward me, but then you'd drive me away again. When we made love I thought I had a chance, but nothing seemed to change afterward."

"I saw you looking at Helen's picture that night, and one of Emma—"

"Emma with you. It was you I was looking at."

"But you seemed troubled. I thought you felt guilty about Helen."

"I was saying goodbye to her. It took me too long to do that, but then there was you, and you filled my heart as no other woman had filled it since she died. I loved you so much Briony, and you wouldn't give an inch."

"*I* wouldn't? It was *you*—" But suddenly it wasn't important anymore. She was laughing and he was laughing with her, and there was nothing in the world but their laughter and joy.

"You kept making me think I had a chance," he told her, "then snatching it away. The night of the party, when you lost your temper with me, you were magnificent, eyes flashing, bosom heaving, I don't know why I didn't pull you down onto the bed and take you there and then."

"Oh, I wish you had," she sighed. "I wanted you so much. I've wanted you all this time, in every way."

He kissed her. "I was ready to murder Denis at Christmas."

"For that innocent little peck under the mistletoe?"

"That innocent little peck nearly sent me off my head. I knew I loved you, but not how much, until I went crazy with jealousy. I discovered that I'm a very jealous, possessive man. You will come home with me tomorrow morning, won't you? You can study business some other way, if you want to. But not here, not away from me."

"Never away from you again, my love. As long as you want me."

"I do want you. But I also have to confess—"

"What is it?"

He grinned. "Emma as good as said that if I didn't get you back I needn't bother coming home."

The laughter welled up out of him and she joined in. "Oh, I'm going to love being her mother," she said, wiping her eyes.

"Why did you leave us? When Emma got better I thought everything was all right, but you couldn't wait to get away—"

"Because I thought you didn't need me anymore. I couldn't live with half measures. It hurt too much."

"I shall always need you, in every way," he said softly, drawing her close to him again. "And I'll prove it every day of my life. Come to me, my love..."

Later he said quietly, "There's something I have to tell you. I didn't know about it myself until yesterday, when Emma told me. When she came round from the operation and said, 'Mummy was there,' she meant much more than we thought."

"She meant Helen," Briony said. "I've always known that."

"Yes, she did. But she meant you, too. I don't fully understand it, but wherever she was, you and Helen were both there. She explained it to me last night. Oswald and Oswald. Mummy and Mummy. To her it's all perfectly simple."

It was the last piece in place, the only thing she needed to hear to make her happiness complete. Briony drew her husband to her—now truly her husband—and gave passionate thanks from the depths of her heart.

They returned home very early the next morning. Dawn was just breaking as the car drew to a halt, and the world was still asleep.

Except for someone at the window above, who vanished as soon as Briony got out of the car and went flying down the stairs and hurled herself into two pairs of waiting arms.

BRIDE'S
BAY RESORT

UNLOCK THE DOOR TO GREAT ROMANCE
AT BRIDE'S BAY RESORT

Join Harlequin's new across-the-lines series, set
in an exclusive hotel on an island off the coast of
South Carolina.

Seven of your favorite authors will bring you exciting stories
about fascinating heroes and heroines discovering love at
Bride's Bay Resort.

Look for these fabulous stories coming to a store near you
beginning in January 1996.

Harlequin American Romance #613 in January
Matchmaking Baby by Cathy Gillen Thacker

Harlequin Presents #1794 in February
Indiscretions by Robyn Donald

Harlequin Intrigue #362 in March
Love and Lies by Dawn Stewardson

Harlequin Romance #3404 in April
Make Believe Engagement by Day Leclaire

Harlequin Temptation #588 in May
Stranger in the Night by Roseanne Williams

Harlequin Superromance #695 in June
Married to a Stranger by Connie Bennett

Harlequin Historicals #324 in July
Dulcie's Gift by Ruth Langan

Visit Bride's Bay Resort each month wherever
Harlequin books are sold.

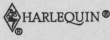

HARLEQUIN ®

BBAYG

Bestselling authors

ELAINE COFFMAN RUTH LANGAN

and

MARY McBRIDE

Together in one fabulous collection!

Available in June wherever Harlequin books are sold.

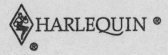

HARLEQUIN ®

OUTB

Harlequin Romance ®

brings you

HOLDING OUT FOR A HERO★

Some men are worth waiting for!

They're handsome, they're charming but, best of all, they're single! Twelve lucky women are about to discover that finding Mr. Right is not a problem—it's holding on to him.

In June the series continues with:

#3411 THE DADDY TRAP
by Leigh Michaels

Hold out for Harlequin Romance's heroes in coming months...

♦ July: **THE BACHELOR'S WEDDING**—Betty Neels

♦ August: **KIT AND THE COWBOY**—Rebecca Winters

♦ September: **REBEL IN DISGUISE**—Lucy Gordon

HOFH-6

❧ *Harlequin Romance* ®
brings you

How the West Was Wooed!

We've rounded up twelve of our most popular authors, and the result is a whole year of romance, Western style. Every month we'll be bringing you a spirited, independent woman whose heart is about to be lassoed by a rugged, handsome, one-hundred-percent cowboy! Watch for...

- June: RUNAWAY WEDDING—Ruth Jean Dale

- July: A RANCH, A RING AND EVERYTHING—Val Daniels

- August: TEMPORARY TEXAN—Heather Allison

- September: SOMETHING OLD, SOMETHING NEW—
  Catherine Leigh

HITCH-5